The
NASCAR-IRANIAN
Connection

Stephen W. Snuffer

Order this book online at www.trafford.com
or email orders@trafford.com

Most Trafford titles are also available at major online book retailers.

Printed in the United States of America.

ISBN: 978-1-4669-1412-4 (sc)
ISBN: 978-1-4669-1411-7 (e)

Library of Congress Control Number: 2012901935

Trafford rev. 02/01/2012

 www.trafford.com

North America & international
toll-free: 1 888 232 4444 (USA & Canada)
phone: 250 383 6864 ♦ fax: 812 355 4082

TABLE OF CONTENTS

DEDICATION

Coach Jerome VanMeter was a great man, known as the Gray Eagle. He took the "board of education" to my backside on several occasions when I got into fights at Beckley Junior High School. In later years, Coach VanMeter saved my life when I ran my motorcycle into a 1956 Chevy and broke my neck. I landed in his front yard on Johnstown Road. The city of Beckley honored Coach VanMeter by naming the local football field in his honor.

Billy Karbonit was the greatest athlete I ever knew. I played baseball with him when he was preparing himself for tryouts with the Pittsburgh Pirates in 1966. He was a football, basketball, and baseball star.

My oldest son, Richard, was a champion baseball and wrestler while in school.

I cannot forget the real heroes, the Navy SEALS. My uncle was a member of what would later become known as SEALS. Many of the lessons I learned in life came from Jimmy Mallamas, one of Ellison's Raders.

Finally, I honor the coal miners who gave their lives on April 5, 2010. At the end of this book is a list of the names of each of these honorable men who died too soon.

This book is dedicated to all of the people I love.

I am called "Wind in the Trees" by my native tribe of Cherokees.

Stephen Wind Snuffer, Author

NOTE: This book is a work of fiction. Rocky VanMeter only lives in the walls surrounding my brain. But, he lives in the hearts of Americans. He is one of those who make America the greatest country in the world. The American spirit is eternal. God bless America and NASCAR drivers! Like Rocky says, "It's like dope; once you try it, you are hooked!"

I hope this book will move you like the wind that moves the trees! I am part Cherokee Indian and my Indian name is "Wind in the Trees."

Please give your support to Special Operations Warrior Foundation. Their contact information is:

Phone: *1-877-337-7693 (Toll free)*
E-Mail: *warrior@specialops.org*

Wounded Warrior Project
      Phone: 1-877-768-6807
      Only $19 per month helps our heroes
      recover their lives after coming home.

Be a hero! Help our heroes!

ABOUT THE AUTHOR

Stephen W. Snuffer graduated from Woodrow Wilson High School in 1967. He is a graduate of Bluefield State College with degrees in law and criminal justice. He also attended Mountain State University and studied paralegal science and did his graduate work in correctional counseling at Marshall University. He has been an owner of a private investigation business called Security 1st in Beckley, West Virginia. He has worked at the State of West Virginia Maximum Correctional Center as a Drug Therapist.

Mr. Snuffer lives on Snuffer Mountain with his wife of 14 years. Together they have five children and nine grandchildren.

He is the author of several books, including:

Mountain Mysteries and Ancient History, Volume I (subtitled "One Tin Soldier Rides Away")

Mountain Mysteries and Ancient History, Volume II (subtitled "Prophecy of the 7th Seal and Crystal Skulls")

Words of Wisdom

Tea Party Factor

His books may be purchased at amazon.com, trafford.com, or xulone.com. Books may be purchased directly from the author by mail. The address is:

Stephen W. Snuffer
PO Box 786
Cool Ridge, WV 25825

"I think that on 9-11, people felt like they did on December 7, 1941 and on November 22, 1963. They felt shock and horror at what our enemies would do and will do. They felt true anger and wanted to fight back. This event brought out the best in the people of the greatest country on the face of the Earth. Let us never forget the threat we face from Iran and terrorists. We must be strong. We need more people like Rocky VanMeter!"

BACKGROUND REPORT ON STEPHEN (SNUFFY) SNUFFER

Stephen "Snuffy" Snuffer entered the military to fly jets. After two years, the military discovered that Snuffy had what they classified as "unique talents." From flying jets, he was transferred into a secret unit. That unit later became known as the "Navy SEALS." His team became known as "SEALS Team Two" and his work was classified. After leaving the military, Snuffy enrolled in law school. Upon graduation, he joined a unique law firm. His clients included ex-presidents, actors, and congressmen.

His last case, which was for the famous Rocky VanMeter, became his most prominent. This book tells that story. Snuffy was hired to represent a NASCAR legend and former Navy SEAL.

In the end, one hero saves another.

p.s. Ghost was Snuffy's SEALS Team 2 partner. After leaving the SEALS, he worked for the FBI in Sterling Park, Virginia. He became an expert with computers, later ran the FBI computer network for the East Coast, moved to the CIA, and headed the network there. He developed connections with the Mob, held a black belt in karate, was an avid motorcycle driver, and became an owner of several fast cars, including a Porsche Panamera. He is considered by many the best of the best in every area of security, investigations, and results.

THE LEGAL TEAM

F. Lee Bailyson, Gerry Spencer, Stephen W. Snuffer, PLLC

Office: 777 Birddog Lane
                     Daytona Beach, FL

Phone: 1-800-LAW-TEAM

Motto: "We Never Lose"

Lead Attorney: Stephen W. Snuffer

Hometown: Beckley, WV

Education: Yale Law School, Harvard Law School, and William & Mary

Specialty: First Degree Murder

Retainer: One million dollars, plus expenses

Requirement: Must not be guilty of accused crime

Legal Rating: Men's Magazine rates Snuffer as the #1 lawyer in the South. He has never lost a case in 25 years of practice.

Car: BMW M5, Blue

Author: Four Books, including:

                 MOUNTAIN MYSTERIES AND ANCIENT HISTORY, VOLUMES 1 AND 2 (trafford.com)

                 THE TEA PARTY FACTOR (amazon.com)

                 THE NASCAR-IRANIAN CONNECTION

PRIVATE INVESTIGATOR

Earl Ray, nickname--"Ghost"

Background: Former Director of International Affairs with the FBI

Former Director of Computer Network Systems for the CIA

Former Navy SEALS Team 2
(Ghost and Snuff were partners)

Training: Black belt in most forms of self-defense

Rating: The Central Times Magazine called Earl Ray "Simply the best at what he does."

Car: Porsche 911, Red

Motorcycle: Suzuki Hayabusa

Side note: *Ghost had three fights in the UFC under an alias name, winning all three fights within the first 60 seconds of the first round, by age 40. Not bad for an old man! Maybe that is why they call him "the Ghost." You never see what's coming until it's too late. It's like he is invisible, like the wind that moves the trees.*

CHAPTER 1

The rolling hills of southern West Virginia show little evidence of the vast deposits of coal lying beneath. Old mine sites dot the countryside. Dead mining towns like Raleigh once housed thousands of miners, who worked 14-hour days, now stand vacant.

Downtown Beckley was the fastest growing city in the East in 1967. The biggest store in town was GC Murphy Company. It was the best-selling store in the company's chain. Now that store has been torn down, replaced by a new federal court building from the President Obama Stimulus. A shovel-ready job where the main business in town is big government, law-enforcement, and lawyers dominate, downtown Beckley. Many businesses have closed up and left. There are many boarded-up store fronts here. Every day at noon, lawyers and judges gather near the big clock on Main Street to talk about business and where they will go for lunch. A lot of pigeons gather on the roof of the Raleigh County Bank overlooking the lawyers. These birds create some shovel-ready jobs, too. The

Raleigh County Courthouse is an old and cramped building dating back to the 1800's. Around it is the usual hodge-podge of county buildings and law offices, the county jail sits on top of the courthouse.

As a small child, I lived beside the Raleigh County Bank, directly across from the courthouse. It was not uncommon to hear screams come from the courthouse as prisoners were taken by way of the elevator up to the jail. Newspaper accounts list the unusual number of suicides in the jail in the late 50's and early 60's, Main Street connects with Kanawha Street. Kanawha Street winds its way south toward MSU (Mountain State University). Mountain State University has had several names over the years; once called Beckley College, then The College of West Virginia, and now Mountain State University. MSU has become the basketball capital of small universities in the East, winning several titles. Their first coach was formerly the local YMCA's basketball coach for the youth team. He took the skills he taught the youth to the next level with a group of college kids all the way to the championships.

Beckley is called "The City of Champions." Sports are big in southern West Virginia. After all, the great Jerry West came from Cabin Creek, a few miles away in Kanawha County. Beckley is known as "The City with a Mine of Its Own." At New River Park, tourists ride in a train through a coal mine that operated in Beckley fifty years ago. John F. Kennedy came to Beckley in 1960 and appeared at the courthouse. The infamous John Edwards came here when he ran for vice-president with John Kerry. Barack Obama came to the Raleigh County Civic Center to campaign for his re-election and attend the funeral of coal miners who were killed at the Upper Big Branch coalmine explosion.

The local newspaper is on North Kanawha Street. It once had two newspapers, the morning and afternoon. The morning paper was Democratic and the evening edition was Republican. It may be said that now the paper is Democratic. I'm not so sure if it can be called fair and balanced. Raleigh County, like most of the state, is Democratic. Some say it's a one-party state. Union membership is high. It has been said that if the devil ran for office with a "D" beside his name, he would be elected because people would assume he was a Democrat.

Children go to Woodrow Wilson High School in Beckley. After graduation, those who cannot afford college go into the coal mines at Eccles or Whitesville. Others take the military route. West Virginia has lost more of its people to war than any other state. Those who are athletes and are lucky, sometimes make it out of West Virginia to professional sports. West Virginia is a pleasant blend of small town southerners and easterners, and a few westerners who earned their living directly or indirectly from coal mining.

The Federal Mine Academy is located in Beaver, West Virginia. Federal mine inspectors from many states are trained here. Many locals trace their background to Native Americans. Throughout West Virginia, under overhanging rock shelters can be found ancient artifacts and burial grounds. Before Columbus came, people from Ireland, Egypt, and other lands, traveled through the hills of West Virginia. An Egyptian urn was found at Sam Black Church on a hill buried seven feet underground by a man building a basement. In Wyoming County, ancient writings were found called Ogam. The writing speaks from the dust of the birth of Jesus Christ. A book called Mountain Mysteries and Ancient History tells of many of the discoveries found in West Virginia. It can be purchased at www.amazon.com. After hundreds of years of mixing races, many of the white folks here have Indian blood. The stigma is fading fast. Indeed, there is now pride in the heritage. My own great-great grandmother was Cherokee. My father's family came to America from Germany. They settled in Pennsylvania and were called Pennsylvania Dutch. Receiving land grants, they ended up in Virginia, now West Virginia, settling at Glen White and Snuffertown. The Bible belt runs hard through Beckley. The town has more than fifty churches from a dozen strains of Christianity, less active today than they once were. There is a Catholic church, a Mormon church (Church of Latter Day Saints), an Episcopalian church, a Seventh Day Adventists church, and a Jewish synagogue. Most claim to be Southern

Baptist. A person's social status is often determined by their religious affiliation.

With about 20,000 people, Beckley is considered by many to be the shopping hub of southern West Virginia. It is located less than 70 miles from the state's capitol in Charleston.

CHAPTER 2

Besides the success of Jerry West, the biggest source of local pride is that of Rocky VanMeter. The local football field was named VanMeter Stadium after him. Rocky was a five-sport letterman at Woodrow Wilson High School. He competed in football, basketball, wrestling, track, and baseball. Some of his records still stand. I recall many football games where he ran the football in for the winning score. In basketball, given the ball with three seconds on the clock, down by one, final shot, nothing but net! I recall the perfect game he pitched at Harry Lewin Field and his own homerun when the score was one to nothing. In track and field, he broke the four-minute mile. As a wrestler, he wins city, country, and state championships. Rocky was unique. While most kids had no idea what they wanted to be when they grew up, Rocky knew. He loved cars and racing on the dirt track at Prosperity. Before graduation, he received scholarship offers from several major universities. Scouts from the Pittsburgh Steelers, Pirates, Bengals, and Reds knocked on his door. All their offers were declined. Opportunity knocked when Bill Francemen called Rocky and he began running at Darlington, South Carolina, on NASCAR's Winston Cup Series. The track is dubbed, "too tough to tame" for its difficulty and ability to turn even the best drivers day into a nightmare. Rocky raced there and the Daytona Beach races. At first, Rocky only made a modest living, for most racing was only a step above being a hobby. When the racing was over, most drivers returned to their day jobs, but not Rocky. He loved the competition and he craved speed. Rocky couldn't afford pilots to fly him to the events, nor could he afford fancy paint schemes, color-coordinated uniforms, or decorative souvenirs. But, with each successive year, NASCAR continued to expand its schedule and Rocky competed, sometimes racing two or three nights in one week. In 1998, he came in second behind Jeff Gordenman. Earlier, in 1995, Jeff was twenty-four, and he won the Winston Cup championship, becoming the youngest driver to do so. Rocky was just twenty years old in 1998 and had hopes of being the youngest yet to win it all.

In 2001, Rocky was near the top of the heap. Then breaking news…"Rocky VanMeter has just announced his retirement from NASCAR! He says his racing career is over!" I still recall the date—September 15, 2001.

CHAPTER 3

DATE: SEPTEMBER 15, 2001

In an exclusive interview given on Gretta's show, she asked Rocky what he would do now. Well, I have decided to go back to southern West Virginia. I need to think. Maybe I will go hunting.

Gretta recalled his rise to NASCAR fame. In 2001, Rocky was climbing the leader board, ranked 5th in points. Only Matt, Tony, Carl, and Kevin had more points. It seemed he was on his way to the top. But, September 11th had changed things. Many thought he was just frustrated at not catching Tony in his last race. He had finished in 5th place in the Chase, 2nd at Talladega, 3rd at Martinsville. He was in the mix with championship hope. At Indy, he finished two one-hundredths of a second behind the winner, Brad. He defeated Jeff a month before at Phoenix International Raceway in the

Nationwide series. One day Rocky was leading the pack, pulling out all the stops. The next day, he tells Gretta he is going hunting in West Virginia...go figure.

Gretta interviewed Kyle, who said Rocky was one of the greatest competitors he had ever known. "This guy has no fear. I've never seen anyone more focused. He is self-motivated on the race track. He has the ability to improve and adapt to the situation. He is so cool and calm under pressure. He is a Mormon; maybe that explains why he is so optimistic. I just don't understand why he quit. It's just not like Rocky to quit anything that he starts. I am at a loss."

Gretta next interviewed Kevin, who said Rocky was the best of the best. "We all looked up to him. He's just the cream of the crop, a great competitor. I think that he may well have won the championship this year. He came close last year. Rocky never quits." "Well, he just did," said Gretta.

Gretta, also spoke with Tony, who said, "Rocky was as hot as they come. He showed no signs of slowing down. He had a real shot with his multiple wins on the board. For God's sake, he won four of the last eight Chase races. He was hot! So, what's up with Rocky? If this is a dream, wake me up! I want another shot at you, man, so get back in the driver's seat!

Joe Gibbson said that he was disappointed. He didn't know where to find a driver like Rocky to replace him. "He's a great competitor. Maybe he just needs some time to sort things out. All I know is that I understand he's going back to the mountains of southern West Virginia. That's where his roots are. Maybe some clean air, some turkey, deer, and bear hunting and some fishing will help him. But, you know Rocky is no quitter; he'll be back. I guarantee it! No one has more skill or more guts on the track. Hell, Rocky reminds me of me!"

"Well, Joe," said Gretta, "you know about his brother, Johnny, right?" "Yes, I know" said Joe. His brother was on the 14th floor of the South Tower. I wish they would stop showing the towers on TV. I mean, I would be upset, too, if I saw my brother jumping out of that building. I mean, how can Rocky help being upset? Those Taliban bastards! If I were younger, I'd sign up to go after those SOB's."

"Well, Joe," said Gretta, "Rocky told me that he was thinking about going into the Navy; maybe even getting into the SEALS program. Maybe he will go hunting for Osama." "Well, God help him if Rocky is on his trail. He'll be the best GD SEAL in the outfit," said Joe. "He'll drive Osama out of his cave. I pity that fool, 'cause you don't want the Rock on your bumper. He'll roll over you and you'll eat his dust. I heard the SEALS turn a boy into a man. Well, Rocky is a man among men. He'll teach those Navy SEALS a thing or two about toughness." "Well folks, that's' our show," said Gretta. "Now, back to you, Shepp!"

CHAPTER 4

DATE: MAY 1, 2011

Eleven years have passed since Rocky left NASCAR.
"Breaking news! Is it really him! He's dead! <u>OSAMA DEAD
TODAY!</u>"

<u>BACKGROUND ON OSAMA BIN LADEN:</u>

*"Osama bin Laden's background emerges from a
fog of vague and often contradictory tales and the
details should be taken with a small helping of
skepticism. The following, however, is a
commonly accepted and reasonable
approximation of the man's background—until a
better story comes along. He was born with
uncertainty, if not conflict, and sometime in the
middle 1950's in Saudi Arabia. His father,
Mohammed bin Laden, had in his lifetime put
together Saudi Arabia's biggest construction*

company, making him and his family prodigiously wealthy. Osama bin Laden was born to one of the last of Mohammed bin Laden's many wives, and he had about fifty siblings. His father died in 1967, leaving Osama independently wealthy.

There are stories that in his late teens, Osama bin Laden lived the life of a playboy in London or Beirut. A more credible story has him attending King Abdul Aziz University, in Jedda, Saudi Arabia, where his belief in Islam became focused into commitment to a radical interpretation of jihad, holy war against the infidels that would bring the world under the rule of ancient Islamic principles.

The Soviet Union gave Osama bin Laden his chance to be a part of the movement by invading Afghanistan in December 1979. Bin Laden joined the Afghan rebels, and at first he used his expertise in the construction industry and his *organizational skills to help refugees who had*

escaped to Pakistan. By 1986, he had made the

personal transition from logistical support to

combat. According to various reports, he and the

Arab unit he led were remarkably brave in the

face of the better-equipped enemy.

As the war in Afghanistan against the Soviet

invaders was nearing the end, bin Laden began

to think globally. In 1988, he formed a new

organization called Al Qaeda, "the military base,"

which counted among its members the leaders of

terrorist organizations and had as its purpose the

worldwide expansion of radical Islamic groups.

The war against the Soviet Union in Afghanistan

ended in 1989 when the Soviet Union withdrew its

forces, but warfare continued as rival Afghan

forces fought for control of what was left of the

country.

In 1990, back in Saudi Arabia, bin Laden thought

he had another righteous cause; the defense of

his country against Iraq, which had invaded its

neighbor Kuwait. He apparently acquired his

hatred for the United States when the Saudi

government chose it rather than him to defend its

country. He was horrified to learn that the

Americans—the infidels, the friend of Israel and

the Jews—would base troops on the sacred soil

that was the site of Islam's holy shrines at Mecca

and Medina.

Bin Laden left his home in Saudi Arabia in April

1991, and after a short stay in Pakistan, he

arrived in Sudan. With the approval of the

Sudanese government, he pursued his two main

interests. He invested in banks, agriculture, and

construction; and under the umbrella of Al Qaeda,

he set up training camps for Islamic warriors. Bin

Laden's revolutionary efforts stretched across

East Africa. His agents set up the blundering

attack in Yemen against American troops on their

way to join the UN task force in Somalia and they

trained the Somalis who were involved in the

notorious "Black Hawk Down" incident that killed

eighteen American soldiers. In 1993, they also

began planning for an attack on the U.S.

embassy in Nairobi, Kenya. The following year,

Saudi Arabia, tiring of bin Laden's militant

escapades, revoked his citizenship.

By 1996, Osama bin Laden's support of terrorist

activities became a concern to the United States

and to Egypt, and both countries pressured

Sudan to expel him, thereby cutting him off from

his business enterprises and his terrorist

infrastructure—or so they thought. Bin laden

returned to Afghanistan in May of that year,

where he was accepted as a guest by the

Taliban, who were consolidating their control of

the country that had been torn apart by tribal

warfare. Far from being neutralized by his

expulsion from Sudan, bin Laden took the

offensive against the country he saw as the

enemy of Islam and God. On August 23, he

issued "The Declaration of Jihad on the

Americans Occupying the Country of the Two

Sacred Placed (Mecca and medina in Saudi

Arabia)." A little more than a month later, the

Taliban drove the remnants of the Afghan

government out of Kabul and declared

themselves the legitimate government of that

country." (Source unknown)

"The latest report said that a team of Special Forces just

raided a residential compound in Abboltagad—5 killed. The

code name of the SEALS Team Six operation was "Geronimo."

A helicopter carrying SEALS Team Six came into a compound

located in Pakistan. Two outside guards were killed by

crossbows from the landing copter. Silent...stealth...deadly.

Commander Rocky VanMeter took out two more as he approached the second floor using his Navy issued silenced 9mm Sig Sauer. He saw Osama peeking out the door—he took a shot"

"Damn!—I missed!" Rocky kicked the door open. The mastermind of 911 grabs a female as a human shield. "I took out her knee with one shot. As she fell to the floor, I took aim with my green laser sight at his head…BANG!—game over. With the help of my team, we placed him in a body bag, gathered papers and his computer, and headed out. The copter failed—set C4 charge—called in second copter. We were out of there before the Pakistan soldiers knew what's happening. Mission accomplished! Took him to the ship; now he's resting with the fishes. Johnny, I did this for you. I know you're in heaven and he is in hell with his ugly unveiled virgins."

General R.T. Darnett debriefs the SEALS and gives them a warning. "We have reason to believe that the Iranians have placed a reward on the heads of every one of you. Watch your back, guys! "In unison, the team shouted, "Sir, yes Sir."

"Dismissed!" shouted the General.

A few days later Rocky and his team are invited to the White House. Gold medals and speeches are given. O'Drama invites Rocky to a White House Beer Summit with Vice President, O'Bryon. The president thanks Rocky for his services to a grateful nation. O'Drama says his poll numbers are up 10 percent. "I think I've got my next election all sewn up now! Rocky, I want you to serve as head of security here in the White House. You will be rewarded beyond your wildest dreams. I'm king of the world."

"Sir, thank you for the offer, but I just want to retire from the military and go home to the southern hills of West Virginia. Just do some hunting and fishing; maybe even go back into NASCAR if they will have an old man, an ex-Navy Seal," said Rocky.

"Well, Rocky, I think the American people will love you no matter what you choose to do. Good luck to you. I wish the

American people loved me as they do you," replied the

President.

CHAPTER 5

In most sports, fans are not allowed to watch teams practice. NASCAR fans get to see it all. They can buy tickets for practice runs. This is when teams test their cars before a race. They also the track to watch qualifying runs. During qualifying, drivers push their cars as fast as they can to compete for the best starting spots on race day. Most races bring between 50,000 and 75,000 fans to the track.

Upon returning to racing, Rocky is often seen signing autographs for fans at trackside. He still remembers where he came from. He's so thankful to be back in the sport he loves. I have traveled to Bristol to watch Rocky since it is not that far away from my home in southern West Virginia. I enjoy the fireworks before the race and during the race, as well. I always wear earplugs because the noise sometimes reaches 130 decibels. Anything over 100 decibels is extremely loud. I gain several pounds when I go to a NASCAR race. I mean, the food just tastes better! The excitement at the track touches everything in some way.

    After the race, Rocky was interviewed by a local TV sports show. "Rocky, why do you worry so much about a few drops of rain on the track. It's really no big deal, is it, Rocky?" He replied, "Well, it's simple, really. Our tires are treadles. Because the tires have no way to channel water away, the moisture forms a thin barrier between the rubber and the road. Let me give you an example. Let's say you cover a of gum or another small flat object with a thin coating of plastic wrap, and then press it down on the bottom of a glass baking dish. Then, try to move the from side to side. The flat, sticky surface of the plastic wrap has formed a tight seal with the glass. This is the same way a treadles tire works on a dry race track. Now, cover the bottom of the glass baking dish with a thin coating of water and try your object again. It's easy to move your of gum around. It's almost impossible to make it stay in one place. Try driving a race car at 170 miles per hour and see what could happen when the track is covered with rain. Now you know why I worry about a little rain!"

Another thing I worry about is the slick stuff. The liquid that no one really wants to see at the track is motor oil from a blown engine. When a motor fails, it sprays oil on the track. Drivers must steer clear of the slick mess. Safety crews must clean it up as quickly as possible. Oil is made to get rid of friction between metal parts on the track. Oil weakens the grip between the tires and the track. So, cars can slide when they drive through spilled oil. After hitting an oil spill, a driver can't do much but hope for the best. No matter how careful drivers are during a race, accidents happen. Drivers know that one drop of oil on a race track can cause a pile up.

The rainbow color design on Rocky's #7 car is the coolest thing on the track. All the drivers like his colors because his #7 is easy to spot. Rocky has followed the trend of using a lot of carbon fiber in the body of his car. He was one of the first guys to use it. He is always ahead of the curve. It's very strong, but light. Each strand of carbon fiber is made up of thousands of very light carbon threads. This gives the material great strength.

Rocky had another first on the track when he started pumping his tires with nitrogen gas instead of air because it has less moisture in it, so it doesn't expand as much as air on hot days. Rocky is always seeking an edge.

CHAPTER 6

"Breaking news! This just in. August 7, 2011."

"Today the nation was horrified as it learned that a CH-47 Chinook helicopter was brought down by an unguided rocket-propelled grenade (RPG) on August 7, 2011. Thirty-eight Special Operation units of Navy SEALS were killed. The RPG was made in Iran and several Iranians were killed in the first fight. The attack highlighted a defensive flaw in US Army helicopters. While they're capable of warding off sophisticated weapons, such as guided missiles, the helos are still susceptible to low-tech attacks from RPG's or small arms fire. Chinooks in Afghanistan have the common missile warning system, which detects radar or infrared guided missiles and spoofs them with chaff (bits of fluttering metal) and flares.

Iran continues its war against American here in Afghanistan, as well as in Iraq. They continue working on the bomb. Our efforts have thus far been unsuccessful in stopping them.

Reports state that five of those killed here were part of the SEALS Team Six that took out Osama. Only one man from that mission remains alive, Commander Rocky VanMeter, now retired and racing cars for NASCAR. An unidentified source stated today that SEALS Team Six completed a classified mission in Iran, which kidnapped three Iranian top scientists and set C4 explosives that set the Iranians back more than a year on their secret atomic program. The source said that a one-million dollar reward was place on the heads of SEALS Team Six. The source also said that they set the SEALS up for this killing. They knew who was coming and waited for them to take off before firing at the Chinook.

"Back to your regular show!"

CHAPTER 7

During a NASCAR race, drivers pass one another at dizzying speeds. The pit crews can decide who wins or loses. They can give the driver precious seconds with a super-fast pit stop that gives them the winning edge. When a driver pulls into the pit, every second counts.

There are six members on the pit crew. Only these six people can hop over the wall that divides the pit area from the track. As fast as they can, the pit crew members put new tires on and pour in more fuel. They also make other necessary changes. Each crew has one jack man, two tire changers, and one gas man.

Every second saved in refueling matters. When drivers pull into the pits, their crews spring into action. Each crew member has a job to do. The job of the gas man is to pour fuel into the tank of the car. A gas man must be very strong. The cans used for refueling hold 12 gallons each. Each can weighs

81 pounds when full. Each car holds 17.5 gallons of fuel.

When the first can is empty, the gas man reaches for another

one. The crew member fills the tank until it is full.

CHAPTER 8

HISTORY OF NASCAR:

The first NASCAR race was held in 1948. Drivers raced on the firm sand of Daytona Beach in Florida. Other tracks were made of dirt. Dirt tracks are still very popular with fans. Red clay is the greatest natural racing surface in the world.

On NASCAR race tracks, the degree of the angles in the corners of the track is knows as banking. Bristol Motor Speedway in Tennessee has a 36 degree bank. Talladega Super Speedway in Alabama has a 33 degree bank. Daytona International Speedway in Florida has a 31 degree bank. The fastest track of the NASCAR circuit is the Texas Motor Speedway in Fort Worth, Texas. Rocky said that Texas is one of his favorites because he likes its high, long turns and new racing surface, which helps cars hold the road.

One of the things that makes Rocky such a great race car driver is when you watch him race through the turns. You can see how great he is at judging the forces of speed and momentum. He uses this skill to race past other drivers coming out of turns. He goes into the turns very fast, and then he slows down rapidly.

The best type of fuel for racing engines has always had a lot of lead. Lead added to gasoline makes an engine perform better. In 2008, all pit crews started using unleaded fuel. In a NASCAR pit stop, a car is filled in ten seconds or so. Before 2008, cars used 22.5 gallons of fuel. The gas man had a very dangerous job. A single spark can ignite racing fuel and create a fire. One gallon can explode with the force of twenty sticks of dynamite.

The fuel cell in a NASCAR vehicle sits behind the driver under the car's trunk. The fuel cell is made of a strong and flexible rubber container called a bladder. Sturdy steel surrounds the bladder. NASCAR fuel cells are designed for safety. They can even survive high speed wrecks. On the top of the gas can is a small valve. This valve controls how much air flows into the can. It also manages how fast the fuel pours out. To understand how the valve works, try this experiment:

1. Fill a glass to the top with water.

2. Put a straw in the water, touching the bottom of the glass.

3. Pinch the top of the straw as hard as you can.

4. Lift the straw above the glass. The water stays inside the straw.

5. Lessen the pressure on the straw to allow a tiny bit of air into the top of the straw. The water will trickle out slowly. Count how long it takes for the straw to empty into the glass.

6. Refill the straw. This time, let the air rush into the straw faster. The water empties into the glass faster than you can count.

The pit crew's gas man has to know exactly how much air to let into the bladder with the fuel.

CHAPTER 9

Today, Rocky celebrated his latest victory at the Infineon Raceway in California. "I owe this victory to my pit crew. I was two laps back, in third place. My crew chief, Donnie Dowell, had talked to me about the importance of saving fuel. This time I remembered his advice. I did not push my car too hard. At the end of the race, I had just enough fuel to finish. I passed the leaders who were running out of gas down the straightaway. I guess you could say Donnie Dowell saved my ass. On my last pit stop my crew replaced all four tires in fourteen seconds. I think that is a record!. This was a team win." declared Rocky.

"The race at Daytona International Speedway in Florida was one of my best races. The crew chief did a great job with my tires. The tires created just the right amount of friction between the tires and the pavement. The right amount of rubber made all the difference in this race. We had to make some major decisions. We had to choose from eighteen different types of rubber blends. The softer tires give more friction and speed, but they wear down faster, so you have to change them more often. We chose the stiffer tires because they last longer. We gave up some speed for durability. We made the right choice on this speedway track."

Rocky continued, "During this race, most of the pit crews used twelve sets of four tires. The cost of each tire is over $500 each. We were able to get by on eleven sets. Do the math, we won! Our pit crew made many changes to help my car run smoothly. The air pressure of each tire makes the difference in how your car handles. We had some problems in the early part of the race, but the crew let out a tiny bit of air in one tire and fixed the problem. Increasing the tire pressure makes tires stiffer. The stiffer tires give a car more spring in the suspension system. A greater spring rate helps a car handle the bumps in a race track better. Your tires make the difference between tenth and first place. The pit crew and

Donnie Dowell won the race. I just drove the car. Great job, guys!"

A tire changer must move quickly during the NASCAR Sprint Cup Challenge—speed is everything. When you are part of a crew, timing is everything. Not every pit stop is the same. Changing all four tires and refueling a near empty tank usually takes sixteen seconds. In the mad dash to beat other cars back onto the track, a crew chief may decide to save time by replacing only the tires on the right side. Near the end of a race, a driver may only get enough fuel to make it to the finish line.

Shared during an interview with MTV Sporting News, "Rocky, tell me what makes your pit crew so special." Rocky responded, "You know, when everything is working right, I can travel about 100 miles before I need more fuel and fresh tires. I communicate with my pit crew and they are ready for my next stop. My crew must decide quickly how to make my car work better. I radio the problems to the crew chief. Everyone knows their job. We only have a few seconds; that often decides who wins and who loses. The job of my crew chief might be the hardest in all of sports. He works twice as many hours as anyone else on the team. He takes the blame when we don't win, but when we win, he has the coolest job around, except for me! I consider every member of my crew family."

"A pit crew has four people who work on the tires and one person who refuels my car. The last crew member who leaps over the wall is my jack man. His job is to lift the car so that the tire changers can work. The 3,400 pound car must go up with just a couple of pumps on each side."

Rocky continued, "Our crew has a fitness program. Every morning you'll see our crew running and lifting weights so that they are strong and fast. They even work on fast speed. Everything is measured not just in tenths of seconds, but thousandths. I call my crew the "A Team." When they are a well-oiled machine, my job is easy. Being a former Navy SEAL, I know what being fit and being a unit means. It can be life or death, winning or losing. I know from combat, you sometimes don't get a second chance to make a first impression. Timing can mean everything in a car race and in life.

CHAPTER 10

MTV Sports interviewed Rocky. "Rocky, tell us more about what your crew chief does." "Well, you know, Donnie Dowell is the best. His job is to get my #7 on the racetrack as quickly as possible. He is the person responsible for making the final decisions. He decides on our team's strategy both on the track and in the pits. He devours information during the race. He knows everything about my car and about me. He also knows a lot about every other car and driver in the race. He knows their strengths and weaknesses; who needs fuel or tires. He knows the track. He can make the difference in a close race. In the race, my pit crew members hop over the wall carrying heavy equipment. They have two 75 pound tires, two 81 pound gas cans, two 5 pound air wrenches, and a 30 pound jack. My crew chief is in charge of preparing the team's car for the race. Once the race begins, he is like the manager of a baseball team. If the team's car is the fastest on the track, the crew chief makes sure that the car doesn't lose time during the race. If the team's car isn't the fastest, the crew chief tries to plan the pit stops perfectly. The crew chief tells the driver when to be patient and when to pass. At the end of the race, the first person a winning driver thanks is his crew chief because he deserves it. My crew chief is always in contact with me on the radio. The only thing he can't do is tell me what's happening around the track. That is the job of my spotter. He watches the race from high above the grandstand. He is calling me on the radio to report accidents and he encourages me in the race. He is a positive force."

"You know, I've been blessed with great Opportunities in life. I believe hard work and determination are keys to getting past the bumps in the road. You can achieve anything in your life that you set your mind to. That's not to say that things will be easy, but you can achieve whatever you really desire to attain."

CHAPTER 11

In the 1930's, a guy named Big Bill France moved to Daytona Beach, where he fell in love with the coast. He was drawn to the beach area where several drivers had made land-speed runs on the hard sand. France was there in 1935 when Sir Malcolm Campbell drove a supercharged V8 rocket named "Bluebird" across the wide sands of Daytona Beach at speeds of 276 mph. Later, Campbell decided the beach wasn't long enough to continue his speed quest, so he moved to Bonneville Salt Flats in Utah, where he continued his record-breaking land speed runs.

There are stories that Junior Johnson was a moonshine hauler. Johnson's daredevil style of driving earned him the nickname, "The Wilkes County Wildman." Junior raced cars for fifty years and became a legend. He ran his first NASCAR race in 1953. He had a record 341 starts, 50 victories, and 71 other top five finishes. He retired in 1966. As a team owner, he had 140 victories and 6 Winston Cup championships.

The first 250-mile beach road race for stock cars was held in Daytona Beach in March 1936. Bill France was among the 27 drivers in the field. Some of the drivers got stuck in the sand; others flipped over. Milt Red Marion won the race. He earned $1700 for the victory. France finished 5th and received $375.

The following year, France staged a race and sold 4500 tickets at 50 cents each. This became the basis for today's NASCAR and the Winston Cup. By the later 1940's, stock car racing began to take off. France's success grew and he decided to create a national championship. On February 21, 1948, NASCAR was incorporated in Daytona Beach, Florida. NASCAR's first sanctioned race was held on Daytona Beach Road course and drew over 10,000 fans.

CHAPTER 12

The foundation for Rocky's love of racing was actually laid 97 years ago when the first races among early production models were held. In fact, racing history may date back to the first two cars and drivers who were willing to race.

Ford's racing history can be traced back to 1901 when founder, Henry Ford, defeated Alexander Winston in a race held in Grosse Pointe, Michigan. From there, auto racing took off.

While motorsports developed worldwide, stock car racing is a uniquely American creation. Its roots are firmly planted in the history of the country, more specifically, the South. It was there that men with time to spare souped up their cars and raced each other.

In the early 1900's, during prohibition, selling alcoholic beverages was banned. Despite these laws against making liquor, an entire hidden industry developed around the country to secretly keep making alcoholic drinks. In West Virginia, we make moonshine. Moonshiners still find a market in southern West Virginia. The town of Mullens still has the good stuff, if you know somebody. Old houses being torn down sometimes have secret rooms where moonshine stills have been found. The moonshiners would hire drivers to run the 'shine throughout West Virginia. The drivers modified cars to allow the liquor to be concealed and to carry as much of the moonshine as possible. They did whatever they could to add additional horsepower so they could outrun the G'men. Prohibition ended in 1933, but moonshiners continue to this very day.

Eventually, local moonshiners began to race each other on oval tracks on vacant farmland. After some time, shrewd businessmen saw a way to make money from these races. The winning driver received a portion of the tickets sold.

CHAPTER 13

The first race under NASCAR's new stock car rules was held on June 19, 1949 in Charlotte, North Carolina. There were more than 13,000 fans on hand. Glenn Dunnaway won the race, but was disqualified because race car inspectors discovered that the 1947 Ford was illegally modified. The inspectors found a wedge jammed in the rear springs of his car, which back then was common in cars used by moonshiners. The wedges stiffened the springs, reduced bounce, and increased the car's speed. Jim Roper finished second in his 1949 Lincoln and was declared champion. He earned $2,000.

In NASCAR's first year, the cars that were used were Lincolns, Caddy's, Oldsmobiles, and Hudsons. There were few modifications back then.

In 1949, NASCAR had eight races. Racing took place at Charlotte, Daytona, Hillsboro, Longhorne, Hamburg, Martinsville, Heidelberg, and Wilkesboro.   NASCAR crowned Red Byron as the first series champ for winning two of eight races. Lee Petty was second. Glenn Dunnaway finished ninth.

In 1950, Bill Reyford of Jamestown, New York, won the NASCAR series championship. Richard Petty, son of Lee, became one of the greatest drivers in NASCAR, winning 200 races. Richard Brickhouse won the first Talladega Superspeedway race in 1968. He received $24,550 for his efforts.

NASCAR staged its last race on dirt in 1970 in Raleigh, North Carolina. Over twenty-two years, and NASCAR had gone from a rag-tag bunch of racers to a serious sport.

In 1971, Bill France retired from running the sport he created. Also in 1971, RJ Reynolds, maker of Winston cigarettes, was the first company to sponsor an entire NASCAR series. Winston Cup is named for RJ.

CHAPTER 14

FIRST NEWS RELEASE:

"Breaking news! August 6, 2011."

"NATO team killed in Afghanistan. Helicopter crash—Taliban and Iranians involved. The Pentagon releases no information on the dead. Navy SEALS operate stealthily throughout Afghanistan."

"In his statement, Karzai said the helicopter went down in Maidan Wardak Province, west of Kabul. According to US officials, killed forces were reinforcing US troops in the single deadliest loss for US troops since the Afghan war began when a helicopter carrying them went down while they were reinforcing…Special Ops forces killed in Wardak Province—22 SEALS dead!"

"It is reported that five or six SEALS who took out Osama were killed in the attack. Early reports say that the

RPG's had Iranian markings on them. Four Iranians were killed in the raid."

CHAPTER 15

"Gentlemen, start your engines!"

"There's the flag! They're off! This could be the race of the year. Rocky VanMeter and Robert Doolittle will be battling for the point to win the chase. Whoever places highest today could just maybe win the championship. Doolittle has the pole, but Rocky is only five spots back. Wow! Look at them go! These guys are going full out at speeds up to 180 mph. In the curve, Doolittle is still in the lead and the rest of the field is right on his ass. Rocky has fallen back to tenth place. It's nip and tuck for the lead. Man, oh man, did you see that! Three laps to go and the flag is out! Four-car pileup in the curve; cars are on fire! I hope nobody got hurt! These cars have a lot of safety features, but….Well, looks like the fire's been put out! The caution flag is out until the debris gets cleaned up off of the track. We'll be back after this message!"

"Doolittle is still in the front as we enter the final lap of the race. Rocky is running second. This is it, folks! Who's going to win it? Wild Bill Robertson is in third place. Final lap,

64

final turn, can Rocky get Doolittle in the final straightaway? A win would give him the points to win the championship."

"What's happened? Doolittle's car has exploded! It's on fire! Metal parts are flying into the air! Oh my God, I don't think there's anything left of Doolittle's car! No one could survive that! Rocky VanMeter managed to pass just before 'KABOOM!' Doolittle's car went up in smoke!   Now that some of the smoke has cleared, I can see that Wild Bill's car has crashed into the wall!"

The fire crews are on the track. God help Robbie Doolittle! He is dead…the king of NASCAR is dead! This is the saddest day in NASCAR history! The race fans are screaming; tears are pouring everywhere! I am speechless. Go to a commercial…."

CHAPTER 16

"Well, there's got to be an investigation. I mean, what really happened here? They check those cars inside out right before the race! Could a spark have hit the fuel line? I think that's not possible the way they design these cars. Safety is of utmost importance. I just can't believe what I just saw!"

"Robby was the best of the best! They called him "The Terminator." Maybe someone terminated him! He bumped a lot of guys out on the track over his years in racing. He had a lot of fist fights! Lots of guys had a reason to take him out, but I think most guys loved the way he raced; most really respected Robby."

"This is a matter for the police now. I guess we should just shut the hell up and let them investigate what happened to Robby's car!"

"This is the end of the show. It's a sad end for the king of NASCAR. The fans have lost their hero. Yes sir, fans have lost the Babe Ruth of professional car racing! I don't think NASCAR will ever find another Robby Doolittle. It's a sad day."

"Holy smoke! Holy smoke! Holy smoke! Robby Doolittle is dead at age 39! Charlotte, North Carolina, is in mourning today! The number three car is no more. Pieces of metal…that's all they can find. They will have to have a closed casket service. They can't find anything but pieces…so sad…so sad! God bless Robert Doolittle and his family. The king is dead! Number 3, Robby Doolittle, the king of NASCAR is dead! He is now in 'racecar heaven.' God has the number 3 car driver in his hands. We will miss him!"

CHAPTER 17

During the investigation, all of the drivers were questioned, as well as the crew chiefs, the pit crew members, and all other employees. Car parts were collected from the racetrack and examined thoroughly. Evidence suggested that a bomb had been sewn into the lining of the Doolittle's car seat.

According to forensics, the car's seat contained residue of C4, an explosive that is not legal to own. This explosive is used by the military, suggesting that someone in the military may have been involved.

The next morning, Rocky and his wife were stopped at the airport. A police dog was called in and his baggage was checked. The dog hit on the bag and it tested positive for explosives. Further examination of Rocky's bag revealed a sock containing a timer on a cell phone. The sock tested positive for C4.

Rocky was taken in to police headquarters and questioned. He was then arrested for the murder of Robert Doolittle. The prosecutor doesn't really want to give Rocky a bond. He tells Judge Barns that no bail should be granted because he was a risk to flee. Because he was an ex-Navy SEAL, he could end up anywhere in the world and we might never find him. I convinced Judge Barns that not setting bail for Rocky was crazy. He was so well-known all over the world and millions of people had seen his face either on television or in person over the last few years, there wouldn't be any place to run. I suggested that Rocky be granted bail and an electronic ankle bracelet be used to track him if he did decide to flee and that Rocky stay at his father's house on John F. Kennedy Drive in Charlotte.

The judge thought long and hard, and then called both of us into his chambers. "Larry, I believe this is an unusual case, but I agree with Mr. Snuffer that there is no place for Mr. VanMeter to run. I mean, as Mr. Snuffer has stated, he's known worldwide. I am therefore going to set bail at one million dollars with the stipulations that an electronic ankle monitor be assigned and that Rocky remain at his father's house. I'll issue an order to the sheriff that Rocky is to be on 24-hour guard there. Mr. VanMeter will be under house arrest. So ordered!"

I thanked the judge. Once the order was completed and signed, I faxed it to the jail so that my client, Rocky VanMeter could be released once his family posted the one-million dollar bond with the court.

Later that afternoon, I met with Rocky. He was concerned and wanted to make sure that I would represent and defend him. He adamantly proclaimed that he was innocent. After hearing his side of the story, I told him that I would take his case, but he had to do things my way and he had to be one-hundred percent upfront and honest with me.

Rocky agreed to my demands and to the one-million dollar retainer. I knew my next step was to get the police reports and any inside information I could. That was the job of the Ghost! Ghost is Earl Ray, my private investigator. He looks like a long-haired hippy with an attitude! I mean, with his long hair and gray beard and driving that red Porsche 911, you think he's a rich yuppie or something! When Ghost is not in his Porsche, he is on his motorcycle. It is a Suzuki Hayabusa. He has his helmet set up with an earpiece and microphone attached to his cell phone. I had to yell because of the loud mixture of wind and the buzz of his motorcycle exhaust blasting in my ears. It's not uncommon for him to run the Charlotte freeway at speeds over 190 mph. He calls it cheating death.

"Can you hear me, Ghost? Ghost, can you hear me?" I yelled.

"Aye-aye, sir! What's happening? I'm just chasing down a Corvette! How about you, Snuffy?" he answered.

"You cheating death today, Ghost? I got a mission for you. I just took on the Rocky VanMeter/Doolittle murder case. I need your Intel,' okay?" I explained.

"What can I do, Snuffy? You know you can count on me," offered Ghost sincerely.

I continued, "Well, police say only three people had a key to the race car garage. Someone planted the C4 in the car. Find out what you can through your sources. Robert Doolittle's key was found at the track in his bag. That leaves the janitor and the crew chief, who says he can't find his key. He thinks maybe he lost it on race day in all that chaos. I want to know everything about the janitor and the crew chief, including their financial backgrounds. I want a full background check on both of them. See what your FBI and CIA sources know and report back to me."

"Okay, Snuffy," said Ghost. "I'm outta here! Catch you later. Got to pass that 'Vette now! Cheat death! Master pain!" shouted Ghost, as the receiver went silent.

Ghost is the best freelance investigator in the world. He spent several years in the FBI and became a computer expert. He was head of the computer systems on the east coast. He then moved up to the CIA. God only knows what he did there. There must be a reason why his nickname is Ghost. He is invisible. I do know one thing. If he is investigating you, you'll

never see him coming 'til he has the scoop on you!

CHAPTER 18

As I was sitting in my office one morning going over the police reports, my cell phone rang. "Hello, it's me; Ghost. I got the scoop on the janitor. His name is Kelly Roland. He has a wife and five kids. When he's not working at the race track, he's preaching at the First Baptist Church. I checked his financial records. He makes $700 a week. Believe it or not, he's debt free. No debts, whatsoever! He has an A1 credit rating. He cleaned up the oil in the garage, but some guy with a thick accent, who said he was a news reporter for the 'Sunday Evening News,' said he was hoping to find a race car driver or pit crew member to interview. Kelly said the track was closed. Kelly wondered how he even managed to get into the garage area. The guy walked away when Kelly tried to talk to him. Kelly said he finished up his cleaning, locked the garage, and left. He checks out clean, Snuffy! He's not your guy." shared Ghost.

"Okay, Ghost, check the crew chief out and get back with me. I'm due in court in fifteen minutes. Oh, wait! Have you thought about putting the baffles back in your motorcycle pipes? You're going to go deaf. Then, what good will you be to me?" I warned.

Ghost replied, "Snuffy, can't do it! Would slow the bike down 10 mph."

"Did you catch the 'Vette yesterday" I asked, remembering the chase that he was on when I spoke with him.

"Yea, he's history!" said Ghost. "He gave me the middle finger when I passed him at 140 mph. Cheap Chevy-Government Motors Crap! I waved at him and shifted gears, ran it up to 175 mph. Still cheating old man Death! Catch you later, Snuffy!"

CHAPTER 19

Later that week, as I was sitting at my desk, my secretary, JoAnn, buzzed me. "Mr. Snuffer, Earl Ray is here to see you."

"Well, send him in, JoAnn!" I exclaimed.

"Ghost, what takes you away from your Busa? Too many bugs in your teeth?" I asked as I reached out to shake his hand.

Ghost answered, "I'm riding my new Panamera. Man, it's so cool! It's a hybrid 3.0 liter, V6. It's got 333 horses under the hood, but will go 0 to 60 in 5.7 seconds! Goes 160 mph top end! Gets 33 miles to the gallon. It's almost as good as the Busa! You've got to see it! Those Germans really know how to build a car; great gas mileage, speed, and it's pretty, too!"

"So, Ghost, you're here to show off your new ride, huh!" I chided him. I knew how much Ghost enjoyed fancy cars and motorcycles, and the faster, the better.

"No, man, I am here to give you the dope on that crew chief, John Doeman," he said.

He had my curiosity. "Okay, so what's up?" I inquired of him.

"Well, he lives high on the hog, and I'm not talking about a v-rod Harley hog! He likes to gamble...Atlantic City...big-time gambler! He owed the mob $250,000. Not as good at cards as he thought he was! Funny thing, though," explained Ghost.

"What's that Ghost?" I needed to hear what he had to say and was becoming very impatient.

"Well, the week before the crash, a lot of pressure was put on him, but three days after the big bang in Charlotte, he pays off his debt in full. Cash, man, green stuff! Where do you want to go next with this, Snuffy?" asked Ghost.

"Let's take the next step. I'll have JoAnn give him a call. We'll give him a choice. Tell him you are investigating this case and you'll be at his home at 9 p.m. tonight. He can let you in and answer our questions or tomorrow we will have papers delivered, signed by the judge." I said.

"Now, let's go see your new toy! Ghost, did you call it a

Panamera?" I asked as we walked out of my office toward the

parking lot.

CHAPTER 20

In law school, I learned how to research court decisions. Students really don't spend much time studying the United States Constitution. It is considered just an old, historic paper. I still believe that the Declaration of Independence was the promise and that the Constitution was the fulfillment.

In the last quarter of the 18th century, no nation in the world was governed with separated and divided powers providing checks and balances on the exercise of authority by those who governed. A first step toward such a result was taken with the Declaration of Independence in 1776, which was followed by the Constitution, drafted in Philadelphia, Pennsylvania, in 1787. In 1791, the Bill of Rights was added. Each document had antecedents back to the Magna Carta and beyond.

The work of fifty-five men at Philadelphia in 1787 was another step toward ending the concept of the divine rights of kings. In place of the absolutism of monarchy, the freedoms flowing from this document created a land of opportunities. Ever since then, discouraged and oppressed people from every part of the world have made their way to our shores. There were others, too—educated, affluent individuals seeking a new life and new freedoms in a new land. This is the meaning of our constitution.

In my defense of Rocky VanMeter, I look to the Constitution to protect him. I intend to protect him under Amendment IV, which says that the right of the people to be secure in their persons, houses, papers, and effects, against unreasonable searches and seizures, shall not be violated. And, no warrants shall be issued, but upon probable cause, supported by oath and particularly describing the place to be searched, and the persons or things to be seized.

Amendment V says that no person shall be held to answer for a capital, or otherwise infamous crime, unless a presentment or indictment of a Grand Jury, except in cases arising in the land or Naval forces, or in the militia…nor shall be compelled to be a witness against himself, nor be deprived of life, liberty, or property without due process of law; nor shall private property be taken for public use without just compensation.

Amendment VI says that in all criminal prosecutions, the accused shall enjoy the right to a speedy and public trial by an impartial jury of the state and district wherein the crime shall have been committed, which district shall have been previously ascertained by law, and to be informed of the nature and cause of the accusation, to be confronted with the witnesses against him, to have compulsory process for obtaining witnesses in his favor, and to have the assistance of counsel for his defense.

Amendment VIII states that excessive bail shall not be required, nor excessive fines imposed, nor cruel and unusual punishments inflicted.

My job is to protect Rocky's rights, to disprove the evidence, which was planted to frame him, and if possible, to discover who had motive to kill the driver or who wanted to put Rocky in jail. Was this government, foreign, or domestic? Was it the military? Was it a NASCAR driver? Was it the White

House? Remember, O'Drama did not want the SEALS to kill

Osama. He wanted him alive to display before the next

election.

CHAPTER 21

In my next meeting with Rocky, he shared more about his time with Navy SEALS Team Six. "Mr. Snuffer, I love hunting and shooting in the hills of southern West Virginia. As a SEAL, I did the job that I was trained to do. It's my job and it's my country that I fight for. If I don't get those bastards, then they kill me! If I don't kill them, then a lot of those young boys dressed up like Marines will die. I reach out with my Winchester and I touch someone! The meek inherit nothing. When the US Navy sends their elite, they send the SEALS Team Six and me. We are the Navy's equivalent to the Israeli Commandos. We practice, but they do! In the SEALS, sometimes we have to face what we try to avoid—our fear of death. As a sniper, I adjust for winds and elevation. My target is from 200 yards to 650 yards away. I rehearse breathing and trigger-touch and pull."

He continued, "In the mud, you learn to forget about the snake at your feet. The more you sweat in practice during peacetime, the less you bleed during war. Things happen so fast! NASCAR is slow in comparison."

I remained silent, listening intently to what Rocky was sharing with me. Rocky continued, "In 1980, after the failed attempt to rescue 53 Americans being held hostage at the US embassy in Iran, the government asked Richard Marcinko to create a new counter-terrorist team and thus they formed SEALS Team Six. I am proud to be one of them--Semper Fi. We train the best and discard the rest! I blame Osama and Iran for the devastation on 911 at Ground Zero. Three thousand good people who did nothing wrong died. One was my brother, Johnny. He led people down to safety and went back up to the 14th floor to look for others to help. He had to jump out the 14th floor to his death. Our Intel' said that Iran was involved. I am glad that I was the one who took out Osama. I am glad that I was on the team that slowed down Iran's atomic bomb program. Can you understand that, Mr. Snuffer?" he asked me.

I shared some of my thoughts with Rocky, and then moved on to other topics. I needed to learn more from him if I was going to stand a chance defending him.

"Rocky, I need to know why your farm has such a sophisticated security system. I mean, what could a retired Navy guy be afraid of?" I inquired.

"Sir, that would be classified," answered Rocky.

"Look, Rocky, you are on trial for your life. I am the only guy that is standing in your corner. What you say to me is also classified. It's called attorney-client privilege. I've got to know about any threats you may be facing; anyone who has some reason to frame you. You must trust me. You're facing a murder rap. I am the only real security you have." I continued. "If you are found guilty, they will put 'Jesus Juice' in your arm, understand?"

Rocky replied, "Sir, this must be kept between you and me." "Rocky, my lips to yours. No taping, nothing on paper, okay?" I promised. "Okay. Well, when I was in the SEALS, our commander ordered us on a Special Ops Mission. We were told that Iran was building an atomic weapon. Sanctions of President O'Drama were not working. We were fighting wars in several countries. Israel was angry with O'Drama because he wanted them to abandon their settlements and to go back to the 1967 boundaries. That said, O'Drama would not give them the code so they could fly planes into Iran to destroy Iran's nuclear facilities. They told us if something wasn't done soon, it would be too late. If Iran had the atomic bomb, they would set the Middle East on fire. We had to do something. Time was of the essence."

"We were ordered to infiltrate the nuclear facility, capture their top scientists, and to use C4 on vital components. We said, 'Aye, aye, Sir,' and I guess we set their program back a couple of years or so. Anyway, a reward of five million dollars was placed on our heads. Iran has spies everywhere, even inside the White House. When that helicopter was taken out by the RPG's, my team died. That was not an accident. They knew who was inside. Anyway, I put in the best security I could find. If you recall, recently they hired a guy out of Mexico to take out the Saudi ambassador in Washington and the Israeli ambassador was also on their list. They will stop at nothing. That's why I set this security system up."

After listening quietly, I told him, "Well, Rocky, if you say you didn't put C4 in that trash can in your barn, then someone else had to. I've got to find out how they got past your security system."

"My wife said the electric went out and the automatic generator system is set to start after ten minutes. Someone could have turned the power off from an electric pole and came to the barn and placed the C4 and timer, and maybe they dropped the glove in a hurry to get out before the security system came back on. That's what I believe happened. Most people are afraid of buffalo. I have a herd of two hundred here. My wife said the German Shepperd barked about 2 a.m. We keep him in the house. My wife heard him bark and got up to look around. That's when she turned the light on, but the light wouldn't work."

Rocky continued, "At the airport, our bags were checked and the timer was found in my socks. They must have entered the hotel when we went to the race. We left at 5 a.m. and did not get back until 9 p.m. We left the next morning at 6 a.m. for the airport."

"Man, I really hope your PI, Ghost, is as good as you claim. This frame looks like it was planned by an expert. Looks like a Special Ops deal. I didn't kill Robby. Yes, we had some trouble last year when he bumped my car. I lost control of the car and hit the wall and broke my wrist. I caught up with him at Victory Lane when he was receiving the trophy and some words were exchanged and he took a swing. I blocked it and countered with my elbow, breaking his nose, but those things just happen in racing. It wasn't really personal. Anyway, that was last year. It wasn't his first fight or mine. Tempers run high in a race."

"Rocky, what can you tell me about your mission in Pakistan on May 1, 2011?" I inquired. "Well, the President waited more than a year before giving the order to get Osama.

We knew where he was, but until O'Drama got into trouble in the polls he would not give the order. I guess Osama was an ace in his hand. Anyway, we were given an order to pick him up!"

I was in shock! "Pick him up?" Rocky continued, "Yes, pick him up. We were to take him alive or our ass would be in a sling. Well, our team thought about it. You might say we discussed what to do. I mean, if we take him alive, the President would apologize to him, set him up for a trial in New York City. Eric Holdshit would find a way to release him or drag out the case for ten years until he died of old age. Anyway, we flipped a coin. It came up heads. Shit happens in Special Operations sometimes. We took him back to the mother-ship and we poured bacon grease over his body and buried him in the sea. No one will ever find his body. The big fish took the bait. I don't know if his followers set me up or the Iranians or someone in NASCAR; could be anyone--politics, the White House—I guess I've got a lot of people who could have set me up."

I couldn't believe the things he was telling me. "Listen, Rocky," I told him, "I want to give you a little background information on Judge Barns, who will be presiding at the trial. He was a high school teacher at one point."

Rocky asked, "What did he teach? And, why is that important?"

"Well," I continued, "he taught English in high school. He couldn't make a living in the legal community. He did some divorce cases and taught some courses at a local community college."

"So, how come he is a judge?" asked Rocky, sounding confused.

"Politics!" I said. "Judge Cauley died and Judge Barns knew someone. That is how judges sometimes get appointed to the court. And, once someone can run on the ballot and put the word 'judge' beside their name, well, they can count on winning the election." I continued, "Rocky, get this! He has been using his new found fame to push the feds to put him on the federal bench! If that happens, then God help the United States of America!"

Rocky spoke up, "Well, why don't you shop for another judge?"

I answered, "Because I wanted him. I can push him a little, get in evidence, and work the jury. If nothing else, I can push for a mistrial or even an appeal. And, besides all of that, he is a NASCAR race fan. He was a Navy man and he has a son in the Marines who is currently stationed in Afghanistan. That could give us an edge. Getting Judge Barns is a gift from heaven, Rocky, trust me!"

CHAPTER 22

"JoAnn, this is Ghost! Patch me through to Snuffy, now! It's important!" yelled Ghost across the telephone line.

"Snuffy, I just left the crew chief in a body bag!" shouted Ghost, sounding out of breath.

"What happened, heart attack?" I asked, wondering what could have possibly happened and if his death may be related to this case.

"Sniper, 500 yards. Couldn't see it coming! I met him at 9 p.m., just as we agreed. I told him we knew about his gambling habits and his debt at Atlantic City and that he was under pressure. I also let him know that he was one of only three people who had a key to the garage. He started to get nervous when I told him we knew he paid it off his gambling debt to the mob in cash three days after his boss was blown into the heavens. I told him we knew he either killed his boss or sold the key to the garage for cash. I told him he had to confess. He was shook up! Was about to break! He was going to spill the beans on who paid him. He just said the words, 'The Iranian...' and then the picture window exploded. The booger-eater got him! Whiskey Tango Foxtrot! The round hit him in the side of the chest, entering on his left and exiting on the right. He convulsed and buckled, falling backward into the wall, then to the floor. I ran outside and fired three shots from my sig 226 into the darkness. Someone threw a flash-bang, stun grenade at me! I took cover and called 911.

"10-18 Urgent Shots Fired!" the words screeched across the radio.

"The police searched the area. Get this, Snuffy! The shot came from 500 yards away!"

"Yea, Ghost, you told me," I said to him.

"Well, anyway, they found the rifle, a Winchester .308 Magnum. No prints on the gun...sniper...rifle had a night vision scope, KN-250. The bullet casing was still in the closed bolt of the gun. They're going to give it to the FBI to check it for prints. I crawled back into the house. I didn't have a blowout kit, but I took my shirt off and covered his wound. Man, they used an armor-piercing bullet, the officer said. He had no chance, no chance at all! Must have been three or four of them because he had to have a spotter, and whoever threw that flash-bang was close. And, maybe even a driver because they were gone quickly. Man, I'm so sorry, Snuffy, I blew this one. I'm usually more careful, Snuffy! I usually scope things out. I guess I'm getting slow. Death was at the door tonight. You know something, Snuffy?"

"What's that, Ghost?" I asked, listening to the cracking in his voice, which was very unusual to hear.

"Well, at times like this, I mean, when you come so close to death that you feel like you can reach out and touch it, that you really feel like you have just somehow cheated death. We are all going to die. When I drive my car on the freeway as fast as I can, or fly on my 'cycle dragging the pegs around a sharp curve at 190 mph, I am on the edge. And, when I survive another day, I think I have cheated him. I laugh when I get past another day, but the truth is, no one cheats death. We walk on a thin dime, waiting for that bump, and death waits for us to fall off," continued Ghost. "You live through it and you laugh! You know that you beat death. But, you know, Snuffy, nobody can beat death. He just waits around the next curve to get you."

"I bet that's how Rocky feels. Hell, that's how I feel. You're more alive in that second than in any other. But, you're right, Ghost! We all try to cheat death. We have no other choice 'til he comes for us for the last time. Problem is, we don't know the moment he will knock on our door," I told him.

Ghost's voice sounded unusual. "You just can't cheat death. Maybe it's not so bad, like good vibrations. Like wind in your face."

"Okay, Snuffy, I gotta go. The police want to know why I am here. They want to see my gun permit. I'm out of here! I'll talk to you later if death doesn't knock on my door!" shouted Ghost.

CHAPTER 23

The trial is held in downtown Charlotte, in the Criminal Court Building in a steel-gray room. If the murder charges are proven, they serve you "Jesus Juice" directly into your arm.

The District Attorney's office has announced that it would seek the death penalty. The case is constructed largely on circumstantial evidence. Rocky has been housed in the men's central jail. Little does he know that a false witness will testify that Rocky told him the he killed Robert Doolittle. This witness is being held on the same floor as Rocky in a high-power module that contained sixteen single prisoner cells that opened out into a dayroom that the prisoners share.

The high-powered detainees have access to the dayroom from 6 a.m. until 6 p.m. The room contains tables where they can eat, play cards, and hang out together if they so choose. According to Terry Darnett, the false witness (liar) who testifies against Rocky, it was at one of these tables that Rocky confessed to him that he committed murder.

The prosecution went out of its way to make Terry Darnett presentable and believable to the jury, which only had three black members. He was given a shave, his hair was taken out of cornrows and trimmed short, and he was dressed in a pale blue suit with matching tie.

In direct testimony elicited by the prosecution, Terry described the conversation he allegedly had with Rocky one morning at one of the tables in the dayroom.

On cross examination, I stood up and took a legal pad with me to the lectern. I am prepared to begin my line of questioning this witness and am determined to uncover his lie.

CHAPTER 24

TRIAL—DAY ONE:

Key Point of Defense Attorney; Snuffer's Law:

"In the practice of law, I have learned that a court room is filled with liars. Lawyers lie and witnesses lie, and the jury has to decide who to believe. A trial is a contest of lies. The judge knows this. Even the jury knows this. They come into the building knowing they will be lied to. They take their seats in the box and agree to be lied to.

My job is to point out those lies so that the jury can see the truth. The trick, if you are sitting at the defense table, is to be patient. I have to wait not just to reveal any lie, but for the lie that I can really grab onto and forge into a knife that cuts through all the crap so everyone can see the truth. That's my job. I take this knife of truth, forge it, and sharpen it. Then at just the right moment, I cut the case open and spill its guts onto the floor so the jury can see through it. It's like lighting a candle in a dark room. When I am finished with the witness, everyone can see his lie and the truth is exposed through the darkness in a place where everybody lies.

The prosecutor, Larry Trailman, brings in his first witness, Terry Darnett.

Mr. Trailman: "Mr. Darnett, do you know Mr. Rocky VanMeter?"

Terry: "Yes, sir, I do."

Mr. Trailman: "How long have you known him?"

Terry: "Well, for years, I guess."

Mr. Trailman: "What do you mean by "for years?"

Terry: "Well, he is famous. I mean he is one of those NASCAR racers on TV."

Mr. Trailman: "Have you ever gone to the speedway here in Charlotte?"

Terry: "No, but I saw him there on TV once. I was in a holding cell when the police brought him in."

Mr. Trailman: "Did you have a conversation with Rocky?"

Terry: "Yes, he told me he killed that race guy, Doolittle.

Mr. Trailman: "Your witness."

Mr. Snuffer: "Mr. Darnett, where did you meet my client?"

Terry: "We met in the holding cell and in the Day Room."

Mr. Snuffer: "Well, then, let's do the math. Rocky was transferred into the jail where you were residing on the 5th of September. Do you remember that?"

Terry: "Yes, I remember him coming in."

Mr. Snuffer: "Why were you in a holding cell?"

The prosecutor stood and objected, saying that I was covering ground he had already brought up in direct testimony. I argued that I was looking for a fuller explanation of Terry's incarceration. Judge Barns allowed me the leeway I needed in my questioning. He instructed Terry to answer the question.

Terry: "Well, the police charged me with a crime."

Mr. Snuffer: "What crime?"

Terry: "They said I stole some stuff during the riot at the

                'Occupy Charlotte Rally.'"

Mr. Snuffer: "Well, Terry, did you steal stuff?"

Terry: "I was in the park. I didn't do anything more than

                anyone else did. Those cops get away with too

                much. They make stuff up about black people to

                get them off the streets."

Mr. Snuffer: "So, Terry, you're innocent of the crime you are

                being charged with?"

Terry: "That's right, man!"

Mr. Snuffer: "Were you looting the store? You are claiming

                that you committed no crime during the riot?"

Mr. Snuffer: "Terry, how much time did you spend with

                Rocky?"

Terry: "Well, about twenty minutes, I guess."

Mr. Snuffer: "Twenty minutes? That's all?"

Terry: "We played cards at the table."

Mr. Snuffer: "Well, Terry, what did you talk about?"

Terry: "I told him I was in here for robbery during the riot. I told him the police are just after black men. We don't have constitutional rights anymore. Look at Rodney King. They beat the hell out of him."

Mr. Snuffer: "Well, Terry, what else was said?"

Terry: "I just ask him why he was in here."

Mr. Snuffer: "What did he say?"

Terry: "He said for murder."

Mr. Snuffer: "Is that all he said?"

Terry: "Well, he said he killed that guy. Yes, that's what he said."

Mr. Snuffer: "Terry, did the prosecutor offer to drop the robbery charge if you testified against Mr. VanMeter today?"

Terry: "No, man, I'm telling the truth. He did it; he told me."

Mr. Snuffer: "So, Terry, a perfect stranger told you that?"

Terry: "Yes, he did. He broke down. He was crying like a baby."

Mr. Snuffer: "Once again, Terry, what will you get from the prosecution if Mr. VanMeter is convicted of this crime? With your prior record, you're looking at two to ten years if you're found guilty of the robbery, right?"

Terry: "I don't know, man. My lawyer takes care of that stuff. Nobody promised me anything."

Mr. Snuffer: "What have you asked the prosecution for in exchange for your testimony? Has your lawyer made a plea bargain?"

Terry: "Nothing, man. I done told you that! I don't know anything about the plea bargaining my lawyer did for me."

Mr. Snuffer: "So, you are not getting anything in exchange for your testimony?"

Terry: "Nothing, man. I tell you the truth."

Mr. Snuffer: "So, then, you are testifying here today because you believe it is your duty as a citizen to testify to the truth, correct?"

Terry: "Yes, sir, that's right. That's just what I am here for, not the plea bargain."

Mr. Snuffer: "Terry, you see this file I am holding? Do you recognize it?"

Terry: "No, never saw it."

Mr. Snuffer: "Terry, are you sure? This file is Rocky's file. Did you look at the contents of that file?"

Terry: "No, not me, man!"

Mr. Snuffer: "I gave that file to Rocky before the bond hearing to read. It contains details of his case. You're sure you didn't take a look at it when Rocky was in the bathroom?"

Terry: "I never did that. You can't prove I did that. I take the 'fifth.' You're not going to get me on that one"

Mr. Snuffer: "Well, Mr. Terry Darnett, did you know that there
              are security cameras in the jail? Do you know
              what the penalty for perjury is, Mr. Darnett?"

Terry: "Man, I plead the 'fifth.' I got nothin' more to say."

From that point on, question after question, Terry
Darnett "took the fifth." I continued my questioning in an effort
to get at the truth.

Mr. Snuffer: "Well, you said you knew my client, Rocky
              VanMeter because you saw him on TV, right?"

Terry: "Yes, sir."

Mr. Snuffer: "So, you contacted the prosecution on October 3rd
              to report his alleged confession."

Terry: "Yes."

Mr. Snuffer: "You are telling me and this jury that a man you
              saw for less than one hour before he was bonded

out broke down and admitted to a perfect stranger that he killed another driver in a race?"

Terry: "Yes, that's what happened."

Mr. Snuffer: "Well, can you tell me again, in Rocky's own words, exactly what he said to you?"

Terry: "He said he ran his car into the guy and his car blew up! That's what he said!"

Mr. Snuffer: "Terry, did you know that Rocky's car was 50 feet ahead of Doolittle's car when it blew up?"

Terry: "No, I didn't."

Mr. Snuffer: "That's all I have. Your witness, Mr. Trailman."

Mr. Trailman: "Nothing further."

CHAPTER 25

TRIAL—DAY TWO:

Questioning continued the next morning, with facts being established and evidence being presented on both sides of the courtroom. Finally, Judge Barns addressed the prosecuting attorney. "Mr. Trailman, will you call your next witness? I want to move forward. It's getting near lunch time.

"Yes, Judge, my next witness is Kelly T. Stump," replied Mr. Trailman. The judged called the witness to the stand and requested that he be sworn in.

Mr. Trailman: "Mr. Stump, please state your name and spell it for the court."

Mr. Stump: "I am Kelly T. Stump. K-E-L-L-Y-T-S-T-U-M-P."

Mr. Trailman: "Mr. Stump, your occupation, please."

Mr. Stump: "I am head of security at the Charlotte County Airport."

Mr. Trailman: "Okay, Mr. Stump, what does your job involve?"

Mr. Stump: "I oversee the baggage that comes into the airport and security of the airport. Nothing gets by me."

Mr. Trailman: "Okay, Mr. Stump, please explain the details of your job and your responsibilities."

Mr. Stump: "Well, we x-ray baggage and look for anything unusual, like contraband."

Mr. Trailman: "What is contraband?"

Mr. Stump: "Anything that could pose a threat to the security of the airport or airplanes. Since 911, we search everything and everyone."

Mr. Trailman: "Well, Mr. Stump, did you inspect Mr. VanMeter's bag?"

Mr. Stump: "Yes. The x-ray machine showed something unusual in Mr. VanMeter's bag."

Mr. Trailman: "Go on!"

Mr. Stump: "Well, like I said, we saw something on the x-ray that gave us pause."

Mr. Trailman: "And, what was that?"

Mr. Stump: "Well, the x-ray indicated that a device was in the bag with two M60 fuses."

Mr. Trailman: "Explain to this jury what you saw."

Mr. Stump: "Well, the shape was like a very small cell phone with some kind of wires attached to two M60 fuses."

Mr. Trailman: "What did you do next?"

Mr. Stump: We asked Mr. VanMeter to step over to the security office and then we opened his bag."

Mr. Trailman: "What did you discover, if anything, in that bag?"

Mr. Stump: "We found a pair of black wool socks and inside one of them was a small cell phone with two M60 fuses attached by wires with a button on it, just like I said we saw in the x-ray."

Mr. Trailman: "Please describe what you did next."

Mr. Stump: "We brought in the explosives dog."

Mr. Trailman: "Did the dog find anything?"

Mr. Stump: "Yes, sir, it hit on the bag, positive for explosives, C4."

Mr. Trailman: "Then what did you do?"

Mr. Stump: "We called the police and explained who we had and what we had found."

Mr. Trailman: "Mr. Stump, what did the police tell you to do next?"

Mr. Stump: They said to be careful and that Mr. VanMeter was a very dangerous man…a Commando…an ex-Navy SEAL. They said they would send a SWAT team. They told us to hold him in a secure facility until they arrived."

Mr. Trailman: "What happened next?"

Mr. Stump: "We received a cell phone call from Officer John Tannamen."

Mr. Trailman: "And, what did he say?"

Mr. Stump: "He told me that the SWAT team was on the roof across the street and to bring Mr. VanMeter out the front door of the airport and to be careful."

Mr. Trailman: "And then what happened?"

Mr. Stump: "We followed the instructions and asked Mr. VanMeter to step outside."

Mr. Trailman: "Did he agree to do as he was asked?"

Mr. Stump: "Yes, Mr. VanMeter agreed to go outside with us."

Mr. Trailman: "Go on. Then what happened?"

Mr. Stump: "Well, Officer Tannamen called out to Mr. VanMeter from behind a police car door and told him to place his hands behind his neck or he would be shot."

Mr. Trailman: "Did he comply?"

Mr. Stump: "At first he kind of looked up and saw the sniper on top of the building across the street with a glass on him. He waited a few seconds, and then did as he was ordered."

Mr. Trailman: "No more questions at this time, Your Honor. Your witness, Mr. Snuffer."

Mr. Snuffer: "Mr. Stump, did Mr. VanMeter cooperate fully with you?"

Mr. Stump: "Yes, he did."

Mr. Snuffer: "Was he alone or with someone else?"

Mr. Stump: 'He was with his wife."

Mr. Snuffer: "How did you know it was his wife?"

Mr. Stump: "Because he said she was his wife. He said they were going home today after winning the NASCAR race yesterday. "Said he missed the Buffalo on his farm in Chillicothe, Ohio."

Mr. Snuffer: "Okay, Mr. Stump, have you ever seen Mr. Rocky VanMeter before?"

Mr. Stump: "Yes."

Mr. Snuffer: "Can you tell the court when you saw him?"

Mr. Stump: "I've watched him race on TV."

Mr. Snuffer: "Just on TV?"

Mr. Stump: "Well, he flies a lot. I have seen him many times at the airport. Hell, he's famous!"

Mr. Snuffer: "Okay, Mr. Stump, did Mr. VanMeter seem surprised when you ask to check his bag?"

Mr. Stump: "Yes, sir."

Mr. Snuffer: "When you pulled the cell phone out of his bag, what did he say?"

Mr. Stump: "He said it wasn't his. He said he had never seen it before."

Mr. Snuffer: "Okay. What did Mr. VanMeter say when the dog hit on his bag?"

Mr. Stump: "He said someone was trying to set him up!"

Mr. Snuffer: "When you asked him to step outside, did he cooperate?"

Mr. Stump: "He said he wanted to call a lawyer."

Mr. Snuffer: "Did he call a lawyer?"

Mr. Stump: "Yes, I guess. He called someone."

Mr. Snuffer: "Who did he call?"

Mr. Stump: "I guess he called you. How would I know?"

Mr. Snuffer: "No further questions at this time."

Judge Barns: Mr. Trailman, call your next witness. Let's move

on this quickly before it's time for lunch. I am

getting hungry."

Mr. Trailman: "Judge, may we take lunch now?"

Judge Barns: "Of course. Adjourned until one o'clock. Jury,

you are dismissed for lunch. I'm out of here!"

CHAPTER 26

After the lunch break, the trial continued with Mr. Trailman calling Wild Bill Robertson to the stand as the next witness. After Mr. Robertson was sworn in, the testimony continued.

Mr. Trailman: "Wild Bill, what do you do for a living?"

Wild Bill: "I am a race car driver with NASCAR."

Mr. Trailman: "Okay, Wild Bill, how long have you been driving on the circuit?"

Wild Bill: "Fifteen years or so, I think. Time flies like speed!"

Mr. Trailman: "So, do you know the defendant, Rocky VanMeter?"

Wild Bill: "Sure! I have raced him for fifteen years, except for when he retired after 911 and went into the service."

Mr. Trailman: "Is he good at what he does?"

Wild Bill: "He's not bad, but not as good as me."

Mr. Trailman: "Okay, Wild Bill, did you know Mr. Robby

Doolittle?"

Wild Bill: "Yes. He was the king. Number 3 was the

greatest!"

Mr. Trailman: "Wild Bill, did you race at the track on the day that

Mr. Doolittle died?"

Wild Bill: "Yea. I was very close to his car going into the

last lap that day."

Mr. Trailman: "So, you saw his car explode?"

Wild Bill: "Yes. I was just behind Rocky and Robby when it

happened. The explosion caused my car to

wreck into the wall."

Mr. Trailman: "Okay, let me ask you this, Wild Bill? Did Rocky

and Robby get along?"

Wild Bill: "What do you mean, 'get along?'"

Mr. Trailman: "Well, did they have any trouble"

Wild Bill: "All drivers have trouble."

Mr. Trailman: "Okay, Wild Bill. What I am asking you is did you ever witness a fight?"

Wild Bill: "Well, Robby liked to bump people out of his way. He has knocked me off of the track more than once."

Mr. Trailman: "Did they ever have a fist fight?"

Wild Bill: "Is the sky blue?"

Mr. Trailman: "Wild Bill, please just answer the question."

Wild Bill: "Well, Robby bumped Rocky's car and he hit the wall. Broke his wrist. That finished his season that year. He and Robby had some words at Victory Circle. Robby threw a punch. You don't throw a punch at an ex-Navy SEAL. Rocky blocked his punch and put his elbow in Robby's nose. Broke it good!"

Mr. Trailman: "So, Wild Bill, you're saying there was blood between them?"

Wild Bill: "I don't think so. They respected each other's

               skills. Guess it was just the heat of the moment.

               Could have happened to anyone out there. Shit

               happens!"

Mr. Trailman: "Thank you, Wild Bill. No further questions."

Judge Barns: "No further questions? Your witness, Mr.

               Snuffer."

Mr. Snuffer: "I have nothing to add. Wild Bill's testimony

               speaks for itself. I even get mad sometimes,

               Judge."

Judge Barns: "That will be enough, Mr. Snuffer. No more

               comments like that one or….Well, you know

               better, right?"

Mr. Snuffer: "Yes, sir. I am sorry, Judge Barns."

Judge Barns: "Mr. Trailman, let's have your next witness,

               unless you want to break for the day. It's already

               two o'clock and I could use a nap."

Mr. Trailman: "Well, if Mr. Snuffer doesn't object, we could call it a day, Your Honor."

Judge Barns: "Mr. Snuffer, I think I've heard enough of you for one day. I think you'll agree with me that it's time to call the cows home, right?"

Mr. Snuffer: "Anything you say, Judge."

Judge Barns: "The jury is excused for the day. See you bright and early tomorrow morning, huh? About 10:30 would be cool. Dismissed!"

CHAPTER 27

At 10:30 the next morning, the trial resumed. "Good morning, ladies and gentlemen." Judge Barns began. "I hope you rested well. It is now 10:30, and we will plan to go until about noon, then go to lunch, and be back here at 1:30. We will recess this evening at 3:00 p.m. Mr. Trailman, your next witness."

Mr. Trailman: "Thank you, Judge. The state calls Eric Wilson."

Judge Barns: "Mr. Wilson, will you be seated and sworn in."

Mr. Trailman: "Okay, Mr. Wilson, you have been sworn in. Will you please tell the court and the jury what you do for a living?"

Eric: "I work for the FBI."

Mr. Trailman: "What do you do for the FBI?"

Eric: "I am an evidence specialist."

Mr. Trailman: "Okay, so were you in charge of the evidence on the day of the explosion at the Charlotte Raceway?"

Eric: "The evidence was gathered and I was in charge of discovery and analyzing what the evidence showed."

Mr. Trailman: "Okay, Mr. Wilson, explain where the evidence led you."

Eric: "Well, inside of the upholstery of the seat of Mr. Doolittle's car, we found residue of C4."

Mr. Trailman: "What is C4?

Eric: "It's a military component used to make bombs."

Mr. Trailman: "Can I go down to Wal-Mart or Lowe's and pick some up?"

Eric: "No, sir! Only governments can issue C4. It's for military use only."

Mr. Trailman: "So, is it your opinion that C4 was the cause of the explosion that killed Mr. Doolittle?"

Eric: "Sure, I am sure of that! About three pounds!"

Mr. Trailman: "In your research and investigation, did you make

                any connection with C4 and Mr. VanMeter?"

Eric: "Yes, sir! Rocky was a Navy SEAL. He was an

                expert with C4 explosives and M60 fuses."

Mr. Trailman: "Judge, no further questions at this time for Mr.

                Wilson."

Judge Barns: "Your witness, Mr. Snuffer."

Mr. Snuffer: "Mr. Wilson, may I call you Eric?"

Eric: "Yes, sir."

Mr. Snuffer: "Eric, how do you know the C4 was buried inside

                of the seat?"

Eric: "NASCAR autos are strictly checked before the

                race and during the race. We found pieces of the

                seat and the chemical used in C4 was traced to

                the seat."

Mr. Snuffer: "Through your investigation, were you able to

                determine the source of that C4?"

Eric: "Yes, sir. It came from Iran."

Mr. Snuffer: "So, how did it get here?"

Eric: "Someone with connections to the Middle East

               brought it to the states."

Mr. Snuffer: "Eric, are you telling us that just because Rocky

               was a Navy SEAL, he has to be the only

               suspect?"

Eric: "No, sir. But, there was C4 residue on his bag at

               the airport."

Mr. Snuffer: "So, that's all you got, right?"

Eric: "No, sir. We had a search warrant issued for

               Rocky's farm at Chillicothe, Ohio and found C4.

               The same type used at the race track was found

               in his barn, hidden in a trash can. We also found

               a timer in his bag at the airport and one in the

               trash can with one glove, which also had C4

               residue on it."

Mr. Snuffer: "Eric, is there anything else you can tell us?"

Eric: "Yes, sir. He has the best security system I've

                 ever seen at his farm. We checked all of his

                 motion detectors and cameras and found that no

                 trespasser came into that barn. It must be his C4,

                 timer, and glove."

Mr. Snuffer: "Well, Eric, as you know, Mr. VanMeter was

                 racing on the day Mr. Doolittle was killed.

                 Nothing was found in his car, so how did he do

                 it?"

Eric: "I don't know. Maybe he had a key to Mr.

                 Doolittle's garage and planted it the night before

                 the race."

Mr. Snuffer: "Well, Mr. VanMeter has an alibi for every minute

                 of the day of the race and for the night before.

                 Explain that to the jury. How did he do it?"

Eric: "We haven't been able to figure that one out yet,

                 but we will in time."

Mr. Snuffer: "Eric, anything else? What about Doolittle's crew

                 chief? Ever think he could have done it?"

Eric: "We will never know. He was dead before we could question him."

Mr. Snuffer: "How did he die?"

Eric: "Three days after the accident, Mr. Earl Ray was conducting an investigation into the accident and was interviewing the crew chief when the crew chief was shot. It happened at about 9:15 p.m."

Mr. Snuffer: "Explain that, sir."

Eric: "Well, the police chief can explain it better."

Mr. Snuffer: "Just tell us what you know."

Eric: "He was shot with a high-powered Winchester .308 rifle, using a 10-power scope with night vision at 500 yards. It was an expert shot!"

Mr. Snuffer: "How do you know the distance and type of rifle?"

Eric: "The police recovered the gun at the scene where it was dropped."

Mr. Snuffer: "Any finger prints?"

Eric: "None on the gun."

Mr. Snuffer: "How about inside of the gun?"

Eric: "Well, the bolt was closed. The police opened it and pulled out a .308 Winchester armor-piercing mag case."

Mr. Snuffer: "What is that?"

Eric: "Well, the case is what holds the powder charge and bullet."

Mr. Snuffer: "Did you find prints on the case?"

Eric: "Yes, sir, a thumbprint."

Mr. Snuffer: "Was it Rocky's thumb print?"

Eric: "Not identified....no."

Mr. Snuffer: "Was there any other evidence at the scene?"

Eric: "Yes. Tire track prints in the muddy field."

Mr. Snuffer: "Mr. Wilson...Eric, excuse me. Do you think my client killed the crew chief?"

Eric: "I don't know, but he was a Navy sniper. He could make such a long shot; he was an expert.

If anyone could make that shot, he knows how to do it."

Mr. Snuffer: "Well, Eric, there is one problem with that."

Eric: "What do you mean?"

Mr. Snuffer: "Three days after Mr. Doolittle died, as you know, Mr. Rocky VanMeter was on house arrest with several cops watching him. He also had an electronic ankle bracelet, which tracked him."

Eric: "Maybe one of his good buddies helped him out. Those SEALS are a tight bunch."

Mr. Snuffer: "One more thing, Eric, what about the tire prints in the mud? Were you able to identify them?"

Eric: "Yes, sir. The prints were from a German sports car, a BMW, maybe one like you drive, Mr. Snuffer."

Mr. Snuffer: "So, you think a county lawyer can shoot that straight?"

Eric: "Don't know. Can you? Were you not a sniper
               for SEALS Team Two before you went to law
               school?"

Mr. Snuffer: "Eric, you're pissing me off!"

Mr. Trailman: "Objection, Your Honor!"

Judge Barns: "Mr. Snuffer, I fine you $1000 for that one. The
               next one will bring jail time. Get it?"

Mr. Snuffer: "Yes, sir. Eric, are you aware that a BMW was
               stopped near the scene just minutes after the
               shooting?"

Eric: "I read the police report of Officer Jones, yes sir."

Mr. Snuffer: "Please tell the jury what that report said."

Eric: "I just recall the time and place where the car was
               pulled over for speeding, 105 mph."

Mr. Snuffer: "What kind of car was it?"

Eric: "It was a German BMW, four-door. There were
               four men inside."

Mr. Snuffer: "Eric, anything else?"

Eric: "The car was two miles north of the site of the shooting at about five minutes from the scene."

Mr. Snuffer: "Did the report identify the men?"

Eric: "The car had DC plates, a black car, four men. The report said they were Iranians, had embassy plates. The officer let them go because they said that they had immunity. The driver tore up the ticket and handed it back to the officer. He was as mad as hell, but he received a call. Shots fired. Go to crew chief's house ASAP! He let them walk...drive, I mean."

Mr. Snuffer: "Your Honor, no further questions at this time."

Judge Barns: "This is a good stopping point for the day. Jury, you are dismissed until tomorrow morning, when we will convene at the usual time. Uh, no, make it 11:00. I need my beauty sleep!"

CHAPTER 28

The next day, the trial did not go forth. I received a call from Judge Barns' law clerk at 6:00 a.m. "The judge wants you in chambers ASAP, Mr. Snuffer," he said.

After arriving at the courthouse, I took the elevator to the third floor. The law clerk pointed to the judge's chambers. I knocked and entered. As I opened the door, the FBI, Eric Wilson, Larry Trailman, and the judge looked at me. Judge Barns peered at me with disdain.

"What?" I asked.

"This case is over, Mr. Snuffer," said Judge Barns. "Give the news to your client."

"What's happened?" I asked in disbelief.

Judge Barns answered, "Here is the list from the FBI, given to me from Eric Wilson ten minutes ago, you lucky SOB! There's no way your defenses would have won this case! There was a car accident at 2 a.m. yesterday on a side street in

Washington, DC. A black BMW was found crashed against a brick wall. The driver was found with his seatbelt wrapped around his neck and his neck was broken. There was no identification in his coat. When the police checked the license plate, they matched it with the BMW that was stopped two miles or so from the crew chief's house the night he was killed. The driver worked as security for the Iranian embassy."

The judge continued, "The list of items recovered from the car's trunk when the police officer opened it. There was a brief case, which contained identification documents of the driver. There were also pictures of Robert Doolittle, his car, his crew chief, Rocky VanMeter, his home and barn, a key to Robert Doolittle's race car garage, two pounds of C4, and a glove with C4 residue on it. The glove matches the glove found at Rocky's barn. A pair of military-style boots was also found in the trunk of the car. An unknown substance on the soles of the boots was sent to the crime lab in Virginia and identified as buffalo manure."

The judge continued, "There were fifty rounds of .308 caliber armor-piercing ammo found and some stun grenades, three flash bangs, an M-49 twenty-power spotting scope, a KN-250 night vision spotter's scope, along with a timer switch and some M60 fuses."

"And, if that weren't enough," said Judge Barns, "the driver's thumbprint matches the print from the .308 Winchester casing found at the sniper's site near the crew chief's house. The tire track casting matches the tires on the BMW M3. The Iranians have no comment! Those damn Iranians have immunity!"

All-in-all, it is clear that this man was the sniper on the hill who killed the crew chief at 500 yards. The Iranian embassy won't even give us the time of day. Looks like a ghost killed him. Justice has been served on this guy."

"In short, Snuffy, we are closing the case against your client. The charges against VanMeter are hereby dropped. Tell your boy he is free to go. You better figure out what you're going to say to the news media. There will be a press conference at 7 a.m. today. Now, Snuffy, get the hell out of my chambers, you lucky SOB! You rich million dollar lawyers make me want to throw up! I do all the work and you get all the glory. They need to put me on the federal court. Hell, I belong on the Supreme Court! Snuffy, I'll see you on TV on the news. Case dismissed!"

"Snuffy, draw up the papers and I'll sign them with prejudices and the case will be stricken from the docket. It is ordered that the bond previously posted in this matter is hereby discharged." he said.

"Judge, all I've got to say about that is Whiskey Tango Foxtrot!," I said as I started toward the door and thought to myself, "This judge has no idea what I just said to him, ha ha! Lazy Judge Barns; God help us if he gets a federal bench appointment!"

CHAPTER 29

After the case was dropped by the FBI evidence, I asked Rocky to meet me at my law office. I wrote myself a check to cover my expenses, the cost of my secretary, and the fee charged by Ghost, my private investigator. I then wrote a refund check to Rocky VanMeter.

When Rocky arrived, I handed him the refund check. "What's this about? It's a check for $950,000!" exclaimed Rocky.

I hesitated, and then said, "You're an American hero and a pretty good driver, Rocky. You fought for America; maybe we helped you, but you saved all of our asses as a SEAL. That's what heroes do! This is your bonus check!"

A few days later, I got a call from Rocky. He asked if I would go to Washington, DC with him on September 11th, and I agreed. We visited the Hero's Wall. After our stop there, we continued on to New York and visited Ground Zero. Rocky was silent..so silent…the sound of silence. Then, he spoke softly.

All I heard was the name, "Johnny." He thanked me. I thanked

him for his service to America—Hooyah!

Rocky came to visit me every year on September 11th. I

could count on getting a call from Rocky, "I'm at the airport at

Beaver," he would say. "Come pick me up!"

The last time I saw him was the week before he died.

As we talked, Rocky recalled how I had told him about my

Uncle Jimmy, one of the first Navy SEALS. He said that he

had something for me to place on Jimmy's grave.

"What is it, Rocky?" I asked. He reached into his pocket

and pulled out his gold medal he had received. As he placed it

in my hand, he said, "It is a medal that the former president

gave me at the 'Beer Summit' at the White House. I want a

real hero to have it. You are my hero for what you did to help

me, and Jimmy was your hero, so you keep it or put it on his

grave--you decide."

"But, Rocky, that is the Presidential Medal of Honor," I

told him. "Are you sure you want to part with it?"

"Yea," said Rocky. "If I had received it from a real American president like Ronald Reagan, it would have been a keeper. But, it was given to me for helping this community organizer get a jump in the poll ratings. It just doesn't have the same meaning. I mean O'Drama doesn't even respect our country or constitution. He thinks he is king!"

"I understand, Rocky," I told him, feeling honored to have known him.

"Listen, if you ever talk to F. Lee again, tell him I said thanks," Rocky said. "We hillbillies have to stick together!"

"Ghost said to tell you hello," I said. "He said that you are his hero!"

Rocky VanMeter never went back to NASCAR. He did go back to his buffalo farm in Chillicothe, Ohio. The last I heard about Rocky was that he went to a class reunion. The television reporter said that he was at the Crossroads Mall in Beckley, West Virginia, and had gone to see a movie with his wife. The movie was about a football hero of the Pittsburg Steelers. The reporter said that he and his beautiful wife sat down in their 911 and Rocky turned the key, then Kaboom! A

C4 explosion! Those damn Iranians! Immunity! I guess they

have a long memory.

The next morning, I turned on FOX news and they had a

breaking news story. Earl Ray was thought to have committed

suicide. His Sig P226 was found in his right hand. He had

been shot between the eyes. Ghost kept his holster on his left

hip! He was left-handed! "You can't cheat death," he had said

so often. So, Rocky is dead, Ghost is dead, and Johnny and

the SEALS team is dead. I think to myself, am I next? I go out

to my new blue BMW M5, get in to go for a ride and think things

over. Do I have the guts to turn the key? Ghost had once said

that the meek shall inherit nothing, because you can't cheat

death. I turn the key. I smell cordite (C4) burning. Kaboom!

CHAPTER 30

"Oh, wow! Oh, wow! Oh, wow! I am amazed! It's like when I stand on the mountain top at Grandview and look down. I am in awe! It is like visiting Sandstone Falls at Hinton or visiting the New River Gorge. I am utterly speechless! I am marveling at the aged mountains that light the countryside like effervescent emeralds and the crystalline creeks that flow like tranquil sonnets. I see the fertile forest and the white-tail deer, the black bear, and the wild turkey. I am being transformed into something else! It's almost heaven. I am back home in West Virginia, Blue Ridge Mountains, Shenandoah River!" I exclaimed.

"Oh, wow! Oh, wow! Oh, wow! Rocky, is that you? Ghost, is that you? I asked in disbelief.

Ghost spoke first. "Yes, Snuffy, we have been waiting for you. And, it's like I always said, you can't cheat death."

142

"Welcome! You're home," said Rocky. "Feel the wind blowing gently against your face? Your heavenly Father is waiting to see you now. Follow us! This is heaven! Snuffy, I this is my brother, Johnny."

"I have heard a lot about you, Johnny. It is an honor to finally meet you. You are truly a hero," I said.

"Snuffy, this is the heaven you looked for within your law books," continued Ghost. "This is one nation under God; indivisible; with liberty and justice for all!"

Rocky spoke again. "Follow us. Jesus Christ, our only King, wants to meet you. The music is so beautiful here! The words sound so sweet and pure."

"Oh, beautiful, for spacious skies; for amber waves of grain. For purple mountains majesty, above the fruited plain! America, America, God shed his grace on thee. And, crown thy good with brotherhood, from sea to shining sea!" Rocky and Ghost sang in unison. "Oh, beautiful, for heroes proved in liberating strife. Who more than self, their country loved, and mercy more than life," they continued at the top of their lungs.

"America, America, may God thy gold refine. Till all success be nobleness, and every gain divine." I joined in, "For patriot dreams that see beyond the years. Thine alabaster cities gleam undimmed by human tears. God shed his grace on thee. And, crown thy good with brotherhood, from sea to shining sea!"

THE END

NAVY SEAL TALK

AC-130 Spectre	Spooky or Puff, the magic dragon
AK-47	Fires a .308 round with an effective range of 330 yards.
AT-4	An 84 mm. One shop light anti-tank rocket.
Agency	CIA—Central Intelligence Agency. Also known as Christians in Action.
Asset	Personnel providing intelligence.
BDU	Battle Dress Uniform
Blowout Kit	Medical pouch
Booger-Eater	Generic term for bad guy.
BS	Bull excrement. Dishonesty.
Cammy	Camouflage
CAR-15	Colt auto-rifle-15. M-16.
CO	Commanding officer.
CQC	Close quarters combat.
Chemlights	Glowsticks
Correct dope	Adjust the scope for windage and distance.
Dam Neck	Dam Neck, Virginia. Home of SEALS Team 6.
Delta Force	Army Commandos.
Dope (Scoop)	Knowledge. Intel. Poop.
E & E	Escape and evasion. Get out of Dodge!
FFP	Final firing position. A sniper's hide from where he fires.
Flashbang	Stun grenade using a nonlethal flash of bright light and loud blast to disorient the enemy.

Full Package	100 men. Birds, Delta snipers, Black Hawks, and Rangers.
Helo	Helicopter.
Humint	Human intelligence
IED	Improvised explosive device
JSOC	Joint Special Ops Command
KIM	Keep in mind
KN-250	Night vision scope
LAW	Light anti-tank weapon. Unguided rocket.
NOD	Night optical device.
OP	Observation post.
OPS	Operations.
P-3 Orion	Navy spy plane.
PJ	Air Force para-rescue Special Ops unit.
PT	Physical training.
QRF	Quick reaction force.
Rangers	Rapid, light infantry unit.
RPG	Rocket-propelled grenade.
SEALS	US Navy Elite Commandos.
SERE	Survival, evasion, resistance, and escape.
Sig Sauer	P-226. Navy 9mm. Made in Germany. Holds 15 rounds. Designed especially for SEALS.
Task Force 160	Night stalkers. Army helicopter unit.
Thermite Grenade	Contains thermite, a chemical that burns at 4,000 degrees Farenheit/2,200 degrees Celcius.
UDT	Underwater demolition team.
Whiskey Tango Foxtrot	WTF. What the F***.

POLICE CODES

10-18	Urgent
10-23	Arrived at scene
10-27	Drivers license information
10-28	Registration information
10-30	Danger
10-32	Units needed
10-33	Emergency
10-35	Fire
10-38	Stopping suspicious vehicle
10-39	Send fire department
10-40	Bomb
10-42	Investigation
10-43	Hazardous materials
10-47	Send medic unit
10-48	Send law enforcement
10-54	Shots fired in area
05	Officer needs help
06A	Accident with injuries
06B	Accident with death
12B	Using guns
17	Suspicious persons
21	Suicide
36	Tampering with auto

NASCAR TRIVIA

According to NASCAR, its events are broadcast in more than 150 countries to 75 million fans. Sponsor advertisements are seen by millions of people who become instant buyers if sponsors have a race team. The car will use their colors and logo. The driver promotes their products. Funds are put into a series purse, making it more exciting for racers and fans. In 2007, payouts were more than $18 million. Racer, Kevin Harvick, received more than $1.5 million for winning one race.

Nextel became sponsor of The Winston Cup Series in 2004. According to NASCAR, Nextel will spend $200 million over a ten-year period to support the series, which is now named The Sprint Cup.

RACETRACKS ON THE NEXTEL CUP SERIES

- Atlanta Motor Speedway
- Bristol Motor Speedway
- California Speedway
- Chicagoland
- Darlington Motor Speedway
- Daytona International Super Speedway
- Dover Downs
- Homestead Motor Speedway
- Indianapolis Motor Speedway
- Infineon Raceway
- Kansas Motor Speedway
- Las Vegas Motor Speedway
- Charlotte Motor Speedway
- Martinsville Speedway
- Michigan Motor Speedway
- New Hampshire Speedway
- Phoenix International Speedway
- Pocono International Speedway
- Richmond International Raceway
- Talladega International Super Speedway
- Texas Motor Speedway
- Watkins Glen International Speedway

NASCAR FIRSTS

First Grand National Race
 June 19, 1949 in Charlotte, NC

First Official Race Winner
 Jim Roper in 1949/Lincoln

First Winner on a Daytona Racetrack
 Red Byron in 1949

First Driver with Four Race Wins in One Season
 Curtis Turner in 1950

First Driver to Win Two NASCAR Championships
 Herb Thomas in 1951 and in 1953

First President to Attend a NASCAR Race
 President Ronald Reagan in 1984

NASCAR FUN FACTS

❖ In 1967, Richard Petty won 27 of 48 races. He also won seven NASCAR titles.

❖ Carl Yarborough won the NASCAR championship three times; 1976, 1977, and 1978. He remained the only driver to win three straight titles.

❖ NASCAR can be summed up in three words:
  ○ Exciting
  ○ Entertaining
  ○ Compelling

❖ NASCAR is a like a drug you get hooked on. (Quote by RockyVan Meter)

❖ Terry Labonte earned more than $1 million from NASCAR in 1984.

❖ Jeff Gordon won seven races in 1992 and earned more than $4.3 million.

❖ In late 1999, NASCAR signed a deal that would pay the race group $2.4 billion.

❖ Rocky VanMeter's greatest racing hero
   was Dale Earnhardt, Sr., driver of the #3
   car, who was bumped, spun, and
   slammed into the wall in Turn 3 of the
   Daytona International Speedway on
   February 18, 2001. His tragic death
   affected millions of fans, who still mourn
   him. He remains one of NASCAR's most
   popular drivers. You cannot go to a race
   without seeing a black #3 displayed
   somewhere.

❖ Rocky VanMeter never raced on the
   anniversary dates of Earnhardt's death to
   honor his memory.

❖ NASCAR's first tracks were all dirt
   surfaces, oval-shaped, and one-half mile
   long. Today's races are run on four types
   of tracks:

   o Tri-oval   Super Speedway
                       (2 miles long)

   o Oval   Speedway or Raceway
                       (1 to 1½ miles long)

   o Short   Short Track
                       (under 1 mile long)

   o Road Course   Twisting Layout
                       (more than 4 turns)

NASCAR'S CHASE FOR THE CUP

Until 2004, NASCAR champions were determined by points earned during all of the races in the season. The driver with the most points at the end of the season won the championship.

In 2004, a new system was started that created a type of playoff system to encourage more an interest. Now, during the first 26 races, drivers earn points for wins, for laps led, and for their finishing position. The top 12 drivers qualify for a special "Chase for the Cup." Their points are reset so that only a few points separate the top 12 positions. During the season's final ten races, these 12 drivers try to earn enough points to end up in the top spot and win what is now called "The Sprint Cup." Once the Chase begins, no other driver but one of these 12 can become the champion, although all of the drivers participate in the final races.

COAL MINERS KILLED AT

UPPER BIG BRANCH MINE ON APRIL 5, 2010

1. *Carl Acord, 52*
2. *Jason Atkins, 25*
3. *Christopher Bell, 33*
4. *Gregory Brock, 47*
5. *Kenneth Chapman, 53*
6. *Robert Clark, 41*
7. *Charles Davis, 51*
8. *Cory Davis, 20*
9. *Michael Ellswick, 56*
10. *William Griffith, 54*
11. *Steven Harrah, 40*
12. *Edward Jones, 50*
13. *Richard Lane, 45*
14. *William Lynch, 59*
15. *Nicholas McCroskey, 26*
16. *Joe Marcum, 57*
17. *Ronald Maynor, 31*
18. *James Mooney, 50*
19. *Adam Morgan, 21*
20. *Rex Mullins, 50*
21. *Joshua Napper, 25*
22. *Howard Payne, 53*
23. *Dillard Persinger, 32*
24. *Joel Price, 55*
25. *Deward Scott, 58*
26. *Gary Quarles, 33*
27. *Grover Skeens, 57*
28. *Benny Willingham, 61*
29. *Ricky Workman, 50*

THE RALEIGH COUNTY COAL MINERS

BY
BRIAN SNUFFER

I'm up early and home late
Providing for my family and doing whatever it takes.
I drive an hour to and from
To get to the mine and get the job done.
When I leave, I'm covered in coal, my face black, my body sore.
But, I get up each morning and give the coal company more.
I'm proud to be a West Virginia coal miner.
'Cause there's not any other job here that is finer.
I went to the mine today and met up with my friends.
We take that long trip and then our journey begins.
It was an ordinary day as we began to work.
But, suddenly the ground beneath our feet shook.
The gases were strong as I began to fall.
I thought of my family and wondered, "Is this all?"
Who will take Bobby to play baseball?
Who will take Sally to the dance hall?
Who will hold my wife when she cries all alone?
I wish I could have said my goodbyes.
Tears roll down my coal-covered face
As my heart begins to race.
Then, all of a sudden I hear a sweet voice.
The mine lights up and I hear a beautiful chorus.
I see an extended hand come my way.
It is covered in coal dust and I wonder who is helping me today.
I grab a'hold and calm fills my soul.
I'm pulled from the ground and out of the coal.
Who is the man who would save me from this?
Who is the hero who gave me a hug and a kiss?
Who is this man covered in coal dust?
Who is this man with his hands pierced with holes and rusty nail dust?
Who is this man who loves me this much?
To pull me out of this coal mine and away from the dust.
I begin to see as I'm pulled out of this mine.
My fellow miners and me, we are all just fine.
They're grinning and laughing, not a worry in sight.
They're walking toward me and into the light.
What took you so long? I heard from another.
We've been waiting on you to get here, my brother.
Don't worry about your family; angels are caring for them. They are alright.
For the man that saved us is holding them tonight.

THE UNITED STATES CONSTITUTION

(See Note 1)

We the People of the United States, in Order to form a more perfect Union, establish Justice, insure domestic Tranquility, provide for the common defence, promote the general Welfare, and secure the Blessings of Liberty to ourselves and our Posterity, do ordain and establish this Constitution for the United States of America.

Article. I.

Section 1.

All legislative Powers herein granted shall be vested in a Congress of the United States, which shall consist of a Senate and House of Representatives.

Section. 2.

Clause 1: The House of Representatives shall be composed of Members chosen every second Year by the People of the several States, and the Electors in each State shall have the Qualifications requisite for Electors of the most numerous Branch of the State Legislature.

Clause 2: No Person shall be a Representative who shall not have attained to the Age of twenty five Years, and been seven Years a Citizen of the United States, and who shall not, when elected, be an Inhabitant of that State in which he shall be chosen.

Clause 3: Representatives and direct Taxes shall be apportioned among the several States which may be included within this Union, according to their respective Numbers, which shall be determined by adding to the whole Number of free Persons, including those bound to Service for a Term of Years, and excluding Indians not taxed, three fifths of all other Persons. *(See Note 2)* The actual Enumeration shall be made within three Years after the first Meeting of the Congress of the United States, and within every subsequent Term of ten Years, in such Manner as they shall by Law direct. The Number of Representatives shall not exceed one for every thirty Thousand, but each State shall have at Least one Representative; and until such enumeration shall be made, the State of New Hampshire shall be entitled to chuse three, Massachusetts eight, Rhode-Island and Providence Plantations one, Connecticut five, New-York six, New Jersey four, Pennsylvania eight,

Delaware one, Maryland six, Virginia ten, North Carolina five, South Carolina five, and Georgia three.

Clause 4: When vacancies happen in the Representation from any State, the Executive Authority thereof shall issue Writs of Election to fill such Vacancies.

Clause 5: The House of Representatives shall chuse their Speaker and other Officers; and shall have the sole Power of Impeachment.

Section. 3.

Clause 1: The Senate of the United States shall be composed of two Senators from each State, chosen by the Legislature thereof, *(See Note 3)* for six Years; and each Senator shall have one Vote.

Clause 2: Immediately after they shall be assembled in Consequence of the first Election, they shall be divided as equally as may be into three Classes. The Seats of the Senators of the first Class shall be vacated at the Expiration of the second Year, of the second Class at the Expiration of the fourth Year, and of the third Class at the Expiration of the sixth Year, so that one third may be chosen every second Year; and if Vacancies happen by Resignation, or otherwise, during the Recess of the Legislature of any State, the Executive thereof may make temporary Appointments until the next Meeting of the Legislature, which shall then fill such Vacancies. *(See Note 4)*

Clause 3: No Person shall be a Senator who shall not have attained to the Age of thirty Years, and been nine Years a Citizen of the United States, and who shall not, when elected, be an Inhabitant of that State for which he shall be chosen.

Clause 4: The Vice President of the United States shall be President of the Senate, but shall have no Vote, unless they be equally divided.

Clause 5: The Senate shall chuse their other Officers, and also a President pro tempore, in the Absence of the Vice President, or when he shall exercise the Office of President of the United States.

Clause 6: The Senate shall have the sole Power to try all Impeachments. When sitting for that Purpose, they shall be on Oath or Affirmation. When the President of the United States is tried, the Chief Justice shall preside: And no Person shall be convicted without the Concurrence of two thirds of the Members present.

Clause 7: Judgment in Cases of Impeachment shall not extend further than to removal from Office, and disqualification to hold and enjoy any Office of honor, Trust or Profit under the United States: but the Party convicted shall nevertheless be liable and subject to Indictment, Trial, Judgment and Punishment, according to Law.

Section. 4.

Clause 1: The Times, Places and Manner of holding Elections for Senators and Representatives, shall be prescribed in each State by the Legislature thereof; but the Congress may at any time by Law make or alter such Regulations, except as to the Places of chusing Senators.

Clause 2: The Congress shall assemble at least once in every Year, and such Meeting shall be on the first Monday in December, *(See Note 5)* unless they shall by Law appoint a different Day.

Section. 5.

Clause 1: Each House shall be the Judge of the Elections, Returns and Qualifications of its own Members, and a Majority of each shall constitute a Quorum to do Business; but a smaller Number may adjourn from day to day, and may be authorized to compel the Attendance of absent Members, in such Manner, and under such Penalties as each House may provide.

Clause 2: Each House may determine the Rules of its Proceedings, punish its Members for disorderly Behaviour, and, with the Concurrence of two thirds, expel a Member.

Clause 3: Each House shall keep a Journal of its Proceedings, and from time to time publish the same, excepting such Parts as may in their Judgment require Secrecy; and the Yeas and Nays of the Members of either House on any question shall, at the Desire of one fifth of those Present, be entered on the Journal.

Clause 4: Neither House, during the Session of Congress, shall, without the Consent of the other, adjourn for more than three days, nor to any other Place than that in which the two Houses shall be sitting.

Section. 6.

Clause 1: The Senators and Representatives shall receive a Compensation for their Services, to be ascertained by Law, and paid out of the Treasury of the United States. *(See Note 6)* They shall in all Cases, except Treason, Felony and Breach of the Peace, beprivileged from Arrest during their Attendance at the Session of their respective Houses, and in going to and returning from the same; and for any Speech or Debate in either House, they shall not be questioned in any other Place.

Clause 2: No Senator or Representative shall, during the Time for which he was elected, be appointed to any civil Office under the Authority of the United States, which shall have been created, or the Emoluments whereof shall have been encreased during such time; and no Person holding any Office under the

United States, shall be a Member of either House during his Continuance in Office.

Section. 7.

Clause 1: All Bills for raising Revenue shall originate in the House of Representatives; but the Senate may propose or concur with Amendments as on other Bills.

Clause 2: Every Bill which shall have passed the House of Representatives and the Senate, shall, before it become a Law, be presented to the President of the United States; If he approve he shall sign it, but if not he shall return it, with his Objections to that House in which it shall have originated, who shall enter the Objections at large on their Journal, and proceed to reconsider it. If after such Reconsideration two thirds of that House shall agree to pass the Bill, it shall be sent, together with the Objections, to the other House, by which it shall likewise be reconsidered, and if approved by two thirds of that House, it shall become a Law. But in all such Cases the Votes of both Houses shall be determined by yeas and Nays, and the Names of the Persons voting for and against the Bill shall be entered on the Journal of each House respectively. If any Bill shall not be returned by the President within ten Days (Sundays excepted) after it shall have been presented to him, the Same shall be a Law, in like Manner as if he had signed it, unless the Congress by their Adjournment prevent its Return, in which Case it shall not be a Law.

Clause 3: Every Order, Resolution, or Vote to which the Concurrence of the Senate and House of Representatives may be necessary (except on a question of Adjournment) shall be presented to the President of the United States; and before the Same shall take Effect, shall be approved by him, or being disapproved by him, shall be repassed by two thirds of the Senate and House of Representatives, according to the Rules and Limitations prescribed in the Case of a Bill.

Section. 8.

Clause 1: The Congress shall have Power To lay and collect Taxes, Duties, Imposts and Excises, to pay the Debts and provide for the common Defence and general Welfare of the United States; but all Duties, Imposts and Excises shall be uniform throughout the United States;

Clause 2: To borrow Money on the credit of the United States;

Clause 3: To regulate Commerce with foreign Nations, and among the several States, and with the Indian Tribes;

Clause 4: To establish an uniform Rule of Naturalization, and uniform Laws on the subject of Bankruptcies throughout the United States;

Clause 5: To coin Money, regulate the Value thereof, and of foreign Coin, and fix the Standard of Weights and Measures;

Clause 6: To provide for the Punishment of counterfeiting the Securities and current Coin of the United States;

Clause 7: To establish Post Offices and post Roads;

Clause 8: To promote the Progress of Science and useful Arts, by securing for limited Times to Authors and Inventors the exclusive Right to their respective Writings and Discoveries;

Clause 9: To constitute Tribunals inferior to the supreme Court;

Clause 10: To define and punish Piracies and Felonies committed on the high Seas, and Offences against the Law of Nations;

Clause 11: To declare War, grant Letters of Marque and Reprisal, and make Rules concerning Captures on Land and Water;

Clause 12: To raise and support Armies, but no Appropriation of Money to that Use shall be for a longer Term than two Years;

Clause 13: To provide and maintain a Navy;

Clause 14: To make Rules for the Government and Regulation of the land and naval Forces;

Clause 15: To provide for calling forth the Militia to execute the Laws of the Union, suppress Insurrections and repel Invasions;

Clause 16: To provide for organizing, arming, and disciplining, the Militia, and for governing such Part of them as may be employed in the Service of the United States, reserving to the States respectively, the Appointment of the Officers, and the Authority of training the Militia according to the discipline prescribed by Congress;

Clause 17: To exercise exclusive Legislation in all Cases whatsoever, over such District (not exceeding ten Miles square) as may, byCession of particular States, and the Acceptance of Congress, become the Seat of the Government of the United States, and to exercise like Authority over all Places purchased by the Consent of the Legislature of the State in which the Same shall be, for the Erection of Forts, Magazines, Arsenals, dock-Yards, and other needful Buildings;--And

Clause 18: To make all Laws which shall be necessary and proper for carrying into Execution the foregoing Powers, and all other Powers vested by this Constitution in the Government of the United States, or in any Department or Officer thereof.

Section. 9.

Clause 1: The Migration or Importation of such Persons as any of the States now existing shall think proper to admit, shall not be prohibited by the Congress prior to the Year one thousand eight hundred and eight, but a Tax or duty may be imposed on such Importation, not exceeding ten dollars for each Person.

Clause 2: The Privilege of the Writ of Habeas Corpus shall not be suspended, unless when in Cases of Rebellion or Invasion the public Safety may require it.

Clause 3: No Bill of Attainder or ex post facto Law shall be passed.

Clause 4: No Capitation, or other direct, Tax shall be laid, unless in Proportion to the Census or Enumeration herein before directed to be taken. *(See Note 7)*

Clause 5: No Tax or Duty shall be laid on Articles exported from any State.

Clause 6: No Preference shall be given by any Regulation of Commerce or Revenue to the Ports of one State over those of another: nor shall Vessels bound to, or from, one State, be obliged to enter, clear, or pay Duties in another.

Clause 7: No Money shall be drawn from the Treasury, but in Consequence of Appropriations made by Law; and a regular Statement and Account of the Receipts and Expenditures of all public Money shall be published from time to time.

Clause 8: No Title of Nobility shall be granted by the United States: And no Person holding any Office of Profit or Trust under them, shall, without the Consent of the Congress, accept of any present, Emolument, Office, or Title, of any kind whatever, from any King, Prince, or foreign State.

Section. 10.

Clause 1: No State shall enter into any Treaty, Alliance, or Confederation; grant Letters of Marque and Reprisal; coin Money; emit Bills of Credit; make any Thing but gold and silver Coin a Tender in Payment of Debts; pass any Bill of Attainder, ex post facto Law, or Law impairing the Obligation of Contracts, or grant any Title of Nobility.

Clause 2: No State shall, without the Consent of the Congress, lay any Imposts or Duties on Imports or Exports, except what may be absolutely necessary for executing it's inspection Laws: and the net Produce of all Duties and Imposts, laid by any State on Imports or Exports, shall be for the Use of the Treasury of the United States; and all such Laws shall be subject to the Revision and Controul of the Congress.

Clause 3: No State shall, without the Consent of Congress, lay any Duty of Tonnage, keep Troops, or Ships of War in time of Peace, enter into any Agreement or Compact with another State, or with a foreign Power, or engage in War, unless actually invaded, or in such imminent Danger as will not admit of delay.

Article. II.

Section. 1.

Clause 1: The executive Power shall be vested in a President of the United States of America. He shall hold his Office during the Term of four Years, and, together with the Vice President, chosen for the same Term, be elected, as follows

Clause 2: Each State shall appoint, in such Manner as the Legislature thereof may direct, a Number of Electors, equal to the whole Number of Senators and Representatives to which the State may be entitled in the Congress: but no Senator or Representative, or Person holding an Office of Trust or Profit under the United States, shall be appointed an Elector.

Clause 3: The Electors shall meet in their respective States, and vote by Ballot for two Persons, of whom one at least shall not be an Inhabitant of the same State with themselves. And they shall make a List of all the Persons voted for, and of the Number of Votes for each; which List they shall sign and certify, and transmit sealed to the Seat of the Government of the United States, directed to the President of the Senate. The President of the Senate shall, in the Presence of the Senate and House of Representatives, open all the Certificates, and the Votes shall then be counted. The Person having the greatest Number of Votes shall be the President, if such Number be a Majority of the whole Number of Electors appointed; and if there be more than one who have such Majority, and have an equal Number of Votes, then the House of Representatives shall immediately chuse by Ballot one of them for President; and if no Person have a Majority, then from the five highest on the List the said House shall in like Manner chuse the President. But in chusing the President, the Votes shall be taken by States, the Representation from each State having one Vote; A quorum for this Purpose shall consist of a Member or Members from two thirds of the States, and a Majority of all the States shall be necessary to a Choice. In every Case, after the Choice of the President, the Person having the greatest Number of Votes of the Electors shall be the Vice President. But if there should remain two or more who have equal Votes, the Senate shall chuse from them by Ballot the Vice President. *(See Note 8)*

Clause 4: The Congress may determine the Time of chusing the Electors, and the Day on which they shall give their Votes; which Day shall be the same throughout the United States.

Clause 5: No Person except a natural born Citizen, or a Citizen of the United States, at the time of the Adoption of this Constitution, shall be eligible to the Office of President; neither shall any Person be eligible to that Office who shall not have attained to the Age of thirty five Years, and been fourteen Years a Resident within the United States.

Clause 6: In Case of the Removal of the President from Office, or of his Death, Resignation, or Inability to discharge the Powers and Duties of the said Office, *(See Note 9)* the Same shall devolve on the VicePresident, and the Congress may by Law provide for the Case of Removal, Death, Resignation or Inability, both of the President and Vice President, declaring what Officer shall then act as President, and such Officer shall act accordingly, until the Disability be removed, or a President shall be elected.

Clause 7: The President shall, at stated Times, receive for his Services, a Compensation, which shall neither be encreased nor diminished during the Period for which he shall have been elected, and he shall not receive within that Period any other Emolument from the United States, or any of them.

Clause 8: Before he enter on the Execution of his Office, he shall take the following Oath or Affirmation:--"I do solemnly swear (or affirm) that I will faithfully execute the Office of President of the United States, and will to the best of my Ability, preserve, protect and defend the Constitution of the United States."

Section. 2.

Clause 1: The President shall be Commander in Chief of the Army and Navy of the United States, and of the Militia of the several States, when called into the actual Service of the United States; he may require the Opinion, in writing, of the principal Officer in each of the executive Departments, upon any Subject relating to the Duties of their respective Offices, and he shall have Power to grant Reprieves and Pardons for Offences against the United States, except in Cases of Impeachment.

Clause 2: He shall have Power, by and with the Advice and Consent of the Senate, to make Treaties, provided two thirds of the Senators present concur; and he shall nominate, and by and with the Advice and Consent of the Senate, shall appoint Ambassadors, other public Ministers and Consuls, Judges of the supreme Court, and all other Officers of the United States, whose Appointments are not herein otherwise provided for, and which shall be established by Law: but the Congress may by Law vest the Appointment of such inferior Officers, as they think proper, in the President alone, in the Courts of Law, or in the Heads of Departments.

Clause 3: The President shall have Power to fill up all Vacancies that may happen during the Recess of the Senate, by granting Commissions which shall expire at the End of their next Session.

Section. 3.

He shall from time to time give to the Congress Information of the State of the Union, and recommend to their Consideration such Measures as he shall judge necessary and expedient; he may, on extraordinary Occasions, convene both Houses, or either of them, and in Case of Disagreement between them, with Respect to the Time of Adjournment, he may adjourn them to such Time as he shall think proper; he shall receive Ambassadors and other public Ministers; he shall take Care that the Laws be faithfully executed, and shall Commission all the Officers of the United States.

Section. 4.

The President, Vice President and all civil Officers of the United States, shall be removed from Office on Impeachment for, and Conviction of, Treason, Bribery, or other high Crimes and Misdemeanors.

Article. III.

Section. 1.

The judicial Power of the United States, shall be vested in one supreme Court, and in such inferior Courts as the Congress may from time to time ordain and establish. The Judges, both of the supreme and inferior Courts, shall hold their Offices during good Behaviour, and shall, at stated Times, receive for their Services, a Compensation, which shall not be diminished during their Continuance in Office.

Section. 2.

Clause 1: The judicial Power shall extend to all Cases, in Law and Equity, arising under this Constitution, the Laws of the United States, and Treaties made, or which shall be made, under their Authority;--to all Cases affecting Ambassadors, other public Ministers and Consuls;--to all Cases of admiralty and maritime Jurisdiction;--to Controversies to which the United States shall be a Party;--to Controversies between two or more States;--between a State and Citizens of another State; *(See Note 10)*--between Citizens of different States, --between Citizens of the same State claiming Lands under Grants of different States, and between a State, or the Citizens thereof, and foreign States, Citizens or Subjects.

Clause 2: In all Cases affecting Ambassadors, other public Ministers and Consuls, and those in which a State shall be Party, the supreme Court shall have original Jurisdiction. In all the other Cases before mentioned, the supreme Court shall have appellate Jurisdiction, both as to Law and Fact, with such Exceptions, and under such Regulations as the Congress shall make.

Clause 3: The Trial of all Crimes, except in Cases of Impeachment, shall be by Jury; and such Trial shall be held in the State where the said Crimes shall have been committed; but when not committed within any State, the Trial shall be at such Place or Places as the Congress may by Law have directed.

Section. 3.

Clause 1: Treason against the United States, shall consist only in levying War against them, or in adhering to their Enemies, giving them Aid and Comfort. No Person shall be convicted of Treason unless on the Testimony of two Witnesses to the same overt Act, or on Confession in open Court.

Clause 2: The Congress shall have Power to declare the Punishment of Treason, but no Attainder of Treason shall work Corruption of Blood, or Forfeiture except during the Life of the Person attainted.

Article. IV.

Section. 1.

Full Faith and Credit shall be given in each State to the public Acts, Records, and judicial Proceedings of every other State. And the Congress may by general Laws prescribe the Manner in which such Acts, Records and Proceedings shall be proved, and the Effect thereof.

Section. 2.

Clause 1: The Citizens of each State shall be entitled to all Privileges and Immunities of Citizens in the several States.

Clause 2: A Person charged in any State with Treason, Felony, or other Crime, who shall flee from Justice, and be found in another State, shall on Demand of the executive Authority of the State from which he fled, be delivered up, to be removed to the State having Jurisdiction of the Crime.

Clause 3: No Person held to Service or Labour in one State, under the Laws thereof, escaping into another, shall, in Consequence of any Law or Regulation therein, be discharged from such Service or Labour, but shall be delivered up on Claim of the Party to whom such Service or Labour may be due. *(See Note 11)*

Section. 3.

Clause 1: New States may be admitted by the Congress into this Union; but no new State shall be formed or erected within the Jurisdiction of any other State; nor any State be formed by the Junction of two or more States, or Parts of States, without the Consent of the Legislatures of the States concerned as well as of the Congress.

Clause 2: The Congress shall have Power to dispose of and make all needful Rules and Regulations respecting the Territory or other Property belonging to the United States; and nothing in this Constitution shall be so construed as to Prejudice any Claims of the United States, or of any particular State.

Section. 4.

The United States shall guarantee to every State in this Union a Republican Form of Government, and shall protect each of them against Invasion; and on Application of the Legislature, or of the Executive (when the Legislature cannot be convened) against domestic Violence.

Article. V.

The Congress, whenever two thirds of both Houses shall deem it necessary, shall propose Amendments to this Constitution, or, on the Application of the Legislatures of two thirds of the several States, shall call a Convention for proposing Amendments, which, in either Case, shall be valid to all Intents and Purposes, as Part of this Constitution, when ratified by the Legislatures of three fourths of the several States, or by Conventions in three fourths thereof, as the one or the other Mode of Ratification may be proposed by the Congress; Provided that no Amendment which may be made prior to the Year One thousand eight hundred and eight shall in any Manner affect the first and fourth Clauses in the Ninth Section of the first Article; and that no State, without its Consent, shall be deprived of its equal Suffrage in the Senate.

Article. VI.

Clause 1: All Debts contracted and Engagements entered into, before the Adoption of this Constitution, shall be as valid against the United States under this Constitution, as under the Confederation.

Clause 2: This Constitution, and the Laws of the United States which shall be made in Pursuance thereof; and all Treaties made, or which shall be made, under the Authority of the United States, shall be the supreme Law of the Land; and the Judges in every State shall be bound thereby, any Thing in the Constitution or Laws of any State to the Contrary notwithstanding.

Clause 3: The Senators and Representatives before mentioned, and the Members of the several State Legislatures, and all executive and judicial Officers, both of the United States and of the several States, shall be bound by Oath or Affirmation, to support this Constitution; but no religious Test shall ever be required as a Qualification to any Office or public Trust under the United States.

Article. VII.

The Ratification of the Conventions of nine States, shall be sufficient for the Establishment of this Constitution between the States so ratifying the Same.

done in Convention by the Unanimous Consent of the States present the Seventeenth Day of September in the Year of our Lord one thousand seven hundred and Eighty seven and of the Independence of the United States of America the Twelfth In witness whereof We have hereunto subscribed our Names,

GO WASHINGTON--Presidt. and deputy from Virginia

[Signed also by the deputies of twelve States.]

Delaware

Geo: Read
Gunning Bedford jun
John Dickinson
Richard Bassett
Jaco: Broom

Maryland

James MCHenry
Dan of ST ThoS. Jenifer
DanL Carroll.

Virginia

John Blair--
James Madison Jr.

North Carolina

WM Blount
RichD. Dobbs Spaight.
Hu Williamson

South Carolina

J. Rutledge
Charles 1ACotesworth Pinckney
Charles Pinckney
Pierce Butler.

Georgia

William Few
Abr Baldwin

New Hampshire

John Langdon
Nicholas Gilman

Massachusetts

Nathaniel Gorham
Rufus King

Connecticut
WM. SamL. Johnson
Roger Sherman

New York

Alexander Hamilton

New Jersey

Wil: Livingston
David Brearley.
WM. Paterson.
Jona: Dayton

Pennsylvania

B Franklin
Thomas Mifflin
RobT Morris
Geo. Clymer
ThoS. FitzSimons
Jared Ingersoll
James Wilson.
Gouv Morris

Attest William Jackson Secretary

NOTES

Note 1: This text of the Constitution follows the engrossed copy signed by Gen. Washington and the deputies from 12 States. The small superior figures preceding the paragraphs designate Clauses, and were not in the original and have no reference to footnotes.

The Constitution was adopted by a convention of the States on September 17, 1787, and was subsequently ratified by the several States, on the following dates: Delaware, December 7, 1787; Pennsylvania, December 12, 1787; New Jersey, December 18, 1787; Georgia, January 2, 1788; Connecticut, January 9, 1788; Massachusetts, February 6, 1788; Maryland, April 28, 1788; South Carolina, May 23, 1788; New Hampshire, June 21, 1788.

Ratification was completed on June 21, 1788.

The Constitution was subsequently ratified by Virginia, June 25, 1788; New York, July 26, 1788; North Carolina, November 21, 1789; Rhode Island, May 29, 1790; and Vermont, January 10, 1791.

In May 1785, a committee of Congress made a report recommending an alteration in the Articles of Confederation, but no action was taken on it, and it was left to the State Legislatures to proceed in the matter. In January 1786, the Legislature of Virginia passed a resolution providing for the appointment of five commissioners, who, or any three of them, should meet such commissioners as might be appointed in the other States of the Union, at a time and place to be agreed upon, to take into consideration the trade of the United States; to consider how far a uniform system in their commercial regulations may be necessary to their common interest and their permanent harmony; and to report to the several States such an act, relative to this great object, as, when ratified by them, will enable the United States in Congress effectually to provide for the same. The Virginia commissioners, after some correspondence, fixed the first Monday in September as the time, and the city of Annapolis as the place for the meeting, but only four other States were represented, viz: Delaware, New York, New Jersey, and Pennsylvania; the commissioners appointed by Massachusetts, New Hampshire, North Carolina, and Rhode Island failed to attend. Under the circumstances of so partial a representation, the commissioners present agreed upon a report, (drawn by Mr. Hamilton, of New York,) expressing their unanimous conviction that it might essentially tend to advance the interests of the Union if the States by which they were respectively delegated would concur, and use their endeavors to procure the concurrence of the other States, in the appointment of commissioners to meet at Philadelphia on the Second Monday of May following, to take into consideration the situation of the United States; to devise such further provisions as should appear to them necessary to render the Constitution of the Federal Government adequate to the exigencies of the Union; and to report such an act for that purpose to the United States in Congress assembled as, when agreed to by them and afterwards confirmed by the Legislatures of every State, would effectually provide for the same.

Congress, on the 21st of February, 1787, adopted a resolution in favor of a convention, and the Legislatures of those States which had not already done so (with the exception of Rhode Island) promptly appointed delegates. On the 25th of May, seven States having convened, George Washington, of Virginia, was unanimously elected President, and the consideration of the proposed constitution was commenced. On the 17th of September, 1787, the Constitution as engrossed and agreed upon was signed by all the members present, except Mr. Gerry of Massachusetts, and Messrs. Mason and Randolph, of Virginia. The president of the convention transmitted it to Congress, with a resolution stating how the proposed Federal Government should be put in operation, and an explanatory letter. Congress, on the 28th of September, 1787, directed the Constitution so framed, with the resolutions and letter concerning the same, to "be transmitted to the several Legislatures in order to be submitted to a convention of delegates chosen in each State by the people thereof, in conformity to the resolves of the convention."

On the 4th of March, 1789, the day which had been fixed for commencing the operations of Government under the new Constitution, it had been ratified by the conventions chosen in each State to consider it, as follows: Delaware, December 7, 1787; Pennsylvania, December 12, 1787; New Jersey, December 18, 1787; Georgia, January 2, 1788; Connecticut, January 9, 1788; Massachusetts, February 6, 1788; Maryland, April 28, 1788; South Carolina, May 23, 1788; New Hampshire, June 21, 1788; Virginia, June 25, 1788; and New York, July 26, 1788.

The President informed Congress, on the 28th of January, 1790, that North Carolina had ratified the Constitution November 21, 1789; and he informed Congress on the 1st of June, 1790, that Rhode Island had ratified the Constitution May 29, 1790. Vermont, in convention, ratified the Constitution January 10, 1791, and was, by an act of Congress approved February 18, 1791, "received and admitted into this Union as a new and entire member of the United States."

Note 2: The part of this Clause relating to the mode of apportionment of representatives among the several States has been affected by Section 2 of amendment XIV, and as to taxes on incomes without apportionment by amendment XVI.

Note 3: This Clause has been affected by Clause 1 of amendment XVII.

Note 4: This Clause has been affected by Clause 2 of amendment XVIII.

Note 5: This Clause has been affected by amendment XX.

Note 6: This Clause has been affected by amendment XXVII.

Note 7: This Clause has been affected by amendment XVI.

Note 8: This Clause has been superseded by amendment XII.

Note 9: This Clause has been affected by amendment XXV.

Note 10: This Clause has been affected by amendment XI.

Note 11: This Clause has been affected by amendment XIII.

This information has been compiled from the U.S. Code. The U.S. Code is published by the Law Revision Counsel of the U.S. House of Representatives.

Updated September 20, 2004

(http://www.house.gov/house/Constitution/Constitution.html)